A Billion-Dollar Family

A bond worth billions!

After graduating from Harvard as best mates, Trace Jackson, Wyatt White and Cade Smith formed the billion-dollar company that made them all superrich. Now life has forced them to go in different directions, but they're still as close as can be.

But while they were successful in business, these tycoons haven't been successful in love...until now. Because they're about to meet the women who will change their lives, and their ideas about family, forever!

Trace heads to Tuscany with the aim of forgetting his past and finds so much more in:

Tuscan Summer with the Billionaire

Stranded in paradise with his ex, Cade must reckon with the secrets that broke them apart in:

The Billionaire's Island Reunion

Single dad Wyatt has a tempting invitation for the woman he's never forgotten in:

The Single Dad's Italian Invitation

Available now!

Dear Reader,

Most of us believe wealthy people have it all. Technically, they do. They can have anything they want. Emphasis on *thing*. But if you really think through their personal interactions, they can be burned more ways than they can be loved.

That was Wyatt White's problem. Except he didn't have to wait until adulthood to realize that having money made his life different, made him a target for people who would take advantage of him. His parents provided that lesson.

At university, he met Trace and Cade, friends who would become his business partners. He watched them fall in love and was happy for them. But he didn't think love was for him.

My favorite kind of character!

I put him in a position where he couldn't dodge the woman of his dreams—or love.

In the final analysis, love comes down to vulnerability and trust. He's a tough character, but Sophie's a formidable heroine. Toss in an adorable baby and Lake Como, Italy, and you have the perfect story to read on a rainy afternoon.

Enjoy!

Susan Meier

The Single Dad's Italian Invitation

Susan Meier

Recycling programs for this product may not exist in your area.

ISBN-13: 978-1-335-40707-8

The Single Dad's Italian Invitation

Copyright © 2022 by Linda Susan Meier

Harlequin Enterprises ULC
22 Adelaide St. West, 41st Floor
Toronto, Ontario M5H 4E3, Canada
www.Harlequin.com

Printed in U.S.A.

Susan Meier is the author of over fifty books for Harlequin. The *Tycoon's Secret Daughter* was a Romance Writers of America RITA® Award finalist, and *Nanny for the Millionaire's Twins* won the Book Buyers Best Award and was a finalist in the National Readers' Choice Awards. Susan is married and has three children. One of eleven children herself, she loves to write about the complexity of families and totally believes in the power of love.

Books by Susan Meier

Harlequin Romance

A Billion-Dollar Family

Tuscan Summer with the Billionaire
The Billionaire's Island Reunion

Christmas at the Harrington Park Hotel

Stolen Kiss with Her Billionaire Boss

The Missing Manhattan Heirs

Cinderella's Billion-Dollar Christmas
The Bodyguard and the Heiress
Hired by the Unexpected Billionaire

Reunited Under the Mistletoe

Visit the Author Profile page
at Harlequin.com for more titles.

Praise for
Susan Meier

"The perfect choice. I read this in one sitting; once I started, I couldn't put it down. *The Bodyguard and the Heiress* will put a smile in your heart. What I love most about Susan Meier's books is the joy your heart feels as you take the journey with characters that come to life. Love this book."

—*Goodreads*

CHAPTER ONE

THE FIRST FRIDAY in June, Wyatt White's limo stopped in front of the Montgomery, one of Manhattan's premiere residences on the Upper East Side. He slid his eight-month-old daughter Darcy out of her car seat. Careful in a way only a single dad knew how to be, he hoped she'd sleep through the jostling while he moved her to the carrier on his chest. But her eyes popped open, and she began screaming again.

"You need a nanny."

Wyatt peered at his business partner, Cade Smith. With thick blond hair and piercing blue eyes, he resembled a surfer more than a businessman, but Cade was shrewd. From the look on his face, Cade had calculated the risk and knew Wyatt couldn't take his sweet baby girl to the upcoming negotiations that Wyatt had to handle.

"No kidding. But I'm wheels up for Lake Como in four hours. That's not enough time to interview and hire someone."

"Call a service."

"I'm not leaving my child with a stranger!"

"The service would vet anybody they sent over. Candidates might be a stranger to you, but not to the service."

"That's the worst argument you've ever made about anything, anywhere, any time."

Cade snorted. "You're too damned picky and it isn't just bad for poor Darcy. It's going to cost us the biggest deal of our lives. Trace will have your head."

Wyatt winced. Trace was the third partner in what they laughingly referred to as Three Musketeers Holdings. And he *would* have Wyatt's head. If Cade was the analyzer, Trace was a fixer. He saw problems and found answers. But Wyatt was the mastermind. He saw opportunity and located the path to get what they wanted and negotiate for it.

Which was why he was the one going to Lake Como to strike the deal with Signor Bonetti to buy his shipping empire.

He had to hope the old guy liked kids. Because he was going to have to bring Darcy with him to their meetings. The only alternative was to leave his baby—his sweet, innocent child— with his stuffy socialite parents. A problem because he'd never told them they had a grandchild. He had enough on his plate adjusting to being a dad. He wasn't ready to add his grouchy parents into the mix.

The limo driver was suddenly at the door, opening it so Wyatt could slide out. Juggling Darcy, her diaper bag and his briefcase, he hoisted himself onto the sidewalk.

Even if it was true that he couldn't keep a nanny because he wanted the best for his child, this was getting old.

He leaned down to be level with the limo door and told Cade, "I'll call you when we get settled."

"I'd rather have you call me when you get a nanny."

The astute driver quickly closed the door to end the conversation and, grateful, Wyatt turned to the Montgomery. Instead of the quiet, sedate building he loved, the place was a beehive of activity. Movers carried furniture and lamps out of the lobby, hauling them to a big box truck.

He squinted at the movers, wondering why they weren't using the service elevator. Then he saw the letters *FBI* printed across the backs of black jackets.

The world stopped for a few seconds. He couldn't hear the blare of taxi horns or Darcy crying. He kept staring at those big white letters.

FBI. Someone in their building had committed a *federal* offense.

That's why they weren't using the service elevator. They were making a statement. Seizing someone's property. Probably hoping the story would be on the six o'clock news.

Darcy amped up the volume of her crying, jerking him back to reality. He rubbed his hand up and down her back. "I'm so sorry, sweetie. I don't know what I'm doing wrong, and you can't tell me. But I'd do anything to help you."

Walking into the lobby with a screaming baby, he knew he was going to have to figure this out soon. Not merely because the FBI commotion seemed to be making his daughter's crying worse, but because he had to negotiate for a shipping company.

"Pete," he called to the doorman across a stack of furniture. "What's going on?"

"You don't know?" Pete shouted to be heard above the baby who had ramped up her crying again.

Guilt that he couldn't settle Darcy raced through him. When she'd been left with him a few months ago, he'd been aces. Now, suddenly, he couldn't get her to stop crying. "I miss a lot lately."

Pete chuckled. "I shouldn't laugh. The building's been full of trouble lately. First, you get a baby you didn't know you had. Then old Mrs. Remirez gets pneumonia. Now, Sophie's been evicted."

Wyatt blinked. "Sophie?"

"Your ex."

That was the problem with living in a five-condo building. It was like a small town. Everybody knew everybody and nobody's business was sacred. "She's being evicted?"

"Not by us. By the FBI. They're seizing her condo. Her mom bought it and pays the HOA fees. Apparently, she's been arrested."

Wyatt squeezed his eyes shut. He and Sophie had met in the lobby the day she'd moved in, and it had been like being struck by lightning. She was tall, beautiful and so funny he'd been captivated. He'd taken her to dinner that night and she'd told him that her mom, owner of a small but growing investment firm, had bought the condo as an investment for a client and needed someone to live in it. Another person might think she'd offered her the condo out of guilt for leaving Sophie with her dad when Sophie was only three. But Sophie assured him her mom had no such feelings. She'd gotten pregnant in a one-night stand and "tried" to make it work with Sophie's dad. When it hadn't, she dropped them both.

If the FBI was seizing a condo supposedly owned by a client of Sophie's mom's, that meant Erica had done something really bad. Maybe even lied about who owned the condo.

He scrubbed his hand across the thick beard on his chin. "Is she gone?"

"Nope. Still up there. She didn't get prior warning, so I'm assuming she's making sure they don't take things she bought herself."

Common sense warred with common decency. It had been three years since he and Sophie had dated. After they broke it off, their schedules were such that they never even bumped into each other in the lobby. Plus, he had a private elevator to the penthouse. They didn't have a connection anymore. It wasn't his job to check up on her.

But he also knew that she'd taken advantage of not needing rent money to cut her work hours in half and enroll in university. She desperately wanted a degree, even if she was starting at twenty-one instead of eighteen, so she'd thrown herself into her studies and she didn't have a lot of friends. Most likely, her mom was in an interrogation room somewhere. Her dad had remarried, had another family, and didn't bother with Sophie much. If Sophie was still in her condo, she was up there alone.

A river of genuine pain for Sophie surged through him. She was the sweetest, nicest, funniest woman he'd ever dated.

And she was alone.

He growled in frustration. With his baby screaming on his chest, he headed for the general elevator. He was not the guy who did missions of mercy. He was the guy who cut deals, grew businesses, made money. How the hell had he become the guy with the baby, who checked up on his old girlfriend?

The elevator bell dinged, and the door opened. He stepped inside. As the doors closed, he looked down at Darcy.

"You wouldn't happen to know if your mother casts spells, creates voodoo dolls…anything like that?"

Darcy only continued to sob.

He tried rubbing her back again. "I'm just saying… I seem to have a lot of weird things happening in my life and she's the only person I know who really hates me… Well, Sophie used to."

Which could potentially turn his checking up on her into an ugly scene.

He took a breath.

It had been three years. She couldn't still be angry. And he couldn't stand the thought that she was facing this alone.

The elevator bell pinged. He stepped out into the hall and walked past the parade of agents carrying Sophie's furniture.

Darcy snuggled against his chest, a move she usually made before she fell asleep, even if it was out of pure exhaustion from sobbing. Simultaneously relieved about Darcy and hesitant about Sophie, he paused at the open door of her condo. Sophie sat on a box in the middle of her empty space, her back to him as she stared out the floor-to-ceiling window. Her long yellow hair was a mass of unruly curls. The T-shirt she wore outlined her slim back.

Attraction and memories hit him like a freight train. He'd been crazy about her. She was funny and soft. Every day with her had been filled with simple fun—

Which was why she'd deserved someone a lot better than a workaholic businessman and a head full of expectations that wouldn't come true. He'd known it. He'd handled it. He'd broken up with her when she started talking as if she expected them to be together forever. She wanted marriage, kids, a house in Connecticut—the trappings of his parents' picture-perfect, fraudulent lives.

She wanted what his parents had. Probably because she didn't know happily-ever-after was a lie.

But he did.

To him, the breakup had been logical, a way to avoid worse pain in the future. He hoped she'd realized that in the three years that had passed and was no longer angry.

He stepped into the empty open-floor-plan area. "Hey."

She turned from the window with a weak smile. When she saw him, her eyes widened before drifting to Darcy.

They hadn't spoken in three years and in that time he'd fathered a baby. The whole building knew the general story, but he'd been careful with the specifics. It was normal that she'd be curious.

"Hey."

"Everything okay?"

She sat up straight, demonstrating her fierce pride. Her mom hadn't wanted her. Her dad struggled to raise her and remarried quickly after she was self-sufficient and basically moved on without her. She had a way of pretending none of that mattered.

"Oh, sure. I mean, it's no thrill being evicted, but this condo was temporary. I knew that."

Because it was an investment for one of her mom's clients. Still, she'd been going to school, hoping to get through enough semesters that finishing would be possible.

When they were together, she'd just begun her freshman year, but she'd lived in this condo the six months they'd dated and three years after that. The stay had lasted a lot longer than she'd thought.

"You only have another semester to get your degree, right?"

She batted her hand. "Don't worry about that."

Hope for her rattled through him. "You finished?"

She shrugged. "No, I have two left. But maybe I don't want to keep going. It was a fluke that my mom showed up with a condo that needed babysitting. With what I know now, I could easily become someone's assistant or maybe manage a coffee shop or something."

He couldn't believe his ears. Where was the formidable woman who could conquer anything? When she'd told him the story of her mom offering her a condo to live in, giving her a chance to get her degree, she'd said she was the luckiest person in the world—

She couldn't possibly want to quit.

"Of course, you should keep going!"

"Look, some people in life are meant to run businesses and make big deals." She smiled briefly. "Like you. Other people like me are meant to be worker bees."

"That's crazy talk. You have a good mind. You have a talent for making people happy and comfortable. You *will* be somebody someday."

"Stop." The optimism she'd been trying to display disappeared from her voice and her pretty face. "I don't need a cheerleader. What I need is to be realistic and I am. I always knew the day would come when I'd have to leave. I was lucky to get over three years here. Now I need to be realistic."

Seeing her brought so low made his chest ache. Even *he* hadn't hurt her this bad. Damn her mother!

He glanced down to make sure Darcy really had fallen asleep. Seeing her softly closed eyes, he strolled a little farther into the room, keeping his voice low and even, almost a whisper. "If it's a matter of money, I could have this condo back in your hands in a few days."

She rolled her eyes and mimicked his lowered voice. "I don't want your charity."

"It wouldn't be charity. I'd buy the condo, let you live here until you finish school, then sell it…probably at a profit. You know how Manhattan real estate is. The longer I keep it, the more I make."

"Did you not hear what you just said? You'd *let* me live here."

Darcy woke with a start. She glanced around the strange environment and released a wail that would have curled Wyatt's toes had they not been in shoes.

Sophie's face crumbled. "I woke her! I'm so sorry!" She bounced off the box. Tall and slim in her faded jeans and bright yellow T-shirt, with elbow-length blond hair that swirled around her when she moved, she took Wyatt's breath away.

He needed a second before he could say, "No. You didn't wake her. She's been like a bear cub with a thorn in its paw for about a week. I have no idea what's wrong."

Sophie eased over. Darcy continued to scream. "How old is she?"

"Eight months or so."

"Does she have any teeth?"

"She's a baby. Babies don't have teeth."

Sophie gaped at him. "Babies can start getting teeth as early as three months." She raced toward the kitchen, washed her hands and dried them in a paper towel, then walked to him again. "Turn her head toward me."

Wyatt did as he was told. Sophie opened Darcy's mouth and stuck a finger inside. "There, there, sweetie. Your daddy's a newbie, but I'm not. I have two half siblings. A sister and a brother. I've been through this." She paused. "Yep. Two teeth coming in on the bottom."

"Really? And it hurts so much that she screams? Why don't I know about this?"

"Why don't you know?" She frowned. "I'd have thought you'd have researched it by now."

Because he was too damned busy with a baby, a job and two partners eager to move into the next phase of their business.

Getting exhausted just thinking about it, he ran his hand along the back of his neck as Sophie continued to run her fingers along Darcy's gums. The scent of her shampoo drifted to him. He could see the light freckling on her pale skin. It had been three years since he'd touched her, yet his palms itched with the memory of how soft she was.

Still rubbing Darcy's gums, Sophie said, "There are two things to know. First, teething is painful, but also it's a strange feeling so it scares her. Second, see how I'm massaging her gums?"

Forcing his mind off his enticing memories of her supple skin, he nodded.

"That sooths the pain. You need some things for her to chew on."

He gaped at her. "Like a chew toy for a dog?"

She sighed. "Sort of but more like a teething ring. You can even get rings you freeze so they do double duty. They give her something to work her gums, even as the ice numbs them. You can find them online or at a drugstore."

Relief rolled through him. "Thank God."

A few seconds of massaging Darcy's gums had calmed her, but Wyatt wasn't fooled. This peace wouldn't last.

Still, he wasn't done with Sophie yet. He might not want what she did out of life, but he'd always liked her. He could help her. If there was one good reason to have money, it had to be the ability to use it to help people.

"Okay. You know I need to go to the drugstore immediately. So don't argue about me buying your condo back from the Feds. Let me do this for you."

Amazed that Wyatt could be so clueless, Sophie Sanders shook her head. It would be a cold, frosty day in hell before she'd let him buy her condo back and *let her* use it. It would be a cold, frosty day before she'd let him do *anything* for her. The tall, dark-haired Adonis, with the neatly trimmed beard that made him look like a sexy stockbroker, had broken her heart into so many pieces she had doubted she'd ever get it back together. There was no way she'd depend on him.

Actually, she was done with depending on anybody. Her dad had a new family. Her mom was a thief and a liar. Even the guy trying to help her had proven himself untrustworthy. So... no. She would be standing on her own two feet from now on.

"I'm fine." *She was fine.* She was twenty-four, almost twenty-five. She had experience waitressing and almost had a degree. Her mom might have let her use the condo, but Sophie had worked for spending money. Yes, she'd be moving out of Manhattan, but there were worse fates.

"Seriously, Wyatt, you don't have to worry about me."

"You are so stubborn!"

"I'm stubborn?" She laughed. "Look, who won't even hire a nanny."

"I've hired plenty of nannies."

"You simply don't keep them." She might not have spoken to Wyatt in the past three years, but a guy didn't get a baby dumped on his doorstep without people talking. She knew one of his former girlfriends had figuratively dropped Darcy in his lap and then gone. Pete had also told her Wyatt hadn't known the ex was pregnant. But he hadn't dodged his responsibilities. Which made his not being able to keep a nanny extremely odd. The doormen even had a betting pool. No nanny ever lasted more than a week, so betters had to choose a day *and* a time the nanny would race through the lobby with all her belongings. The winner was the person who picked the day and time closest to when Wyatt fired her.

"There's always something about them that isn't quite right." He glanced down at Darcy, then back at Sophie. "She's still not screaming."

"The massage will last a bit. It would last even longer if you would go to the drugstore already and get one of those teething rings that I told you about."

His eyes narrowed. His expression shifted. She

knew the look. He was calculating something in his head. "You learned all this from helping with your brother and sister?"

"I lived with them for two years after my dad got married, from sixteen to eighteen when I moved out." She shrugged. "I picked up some stuff just watching my stepmom."

"You know a lot about kids?"

She frowned. "I know a *bit* about *babies*."

"I leave this afternoon for Lake Como, Italy. I'll be there for the next two weeks or so, negotiating to buy a company. I suspect it will take ten days, but we have the extra four just in case."

Surprised by the change of subject, she peered at him. "Bragging or complaining?"

"I desperately need someone to come with me to help with Darcy. I can't take her to negotiations." He winced. "I mean, I could. I've done it off and on for months… But this deal is important."

Suddenly his calculating expression made sense. "Are you asking me to come with you to take care of your child?"

He winced again. "I know. It really sounds awful of me, but you need cash and a place to stay, and I need someone to care for Darcy." He took a breath. "I would pay you handsomely. *Pay* you. For your *help*. This wouldn't be charity."

She said nothing, even though the money she

could make would be a huge plus in terms of getting a new apartment, since it might be enough for a security deposit.

He shook his head. "We leave in four hours. I'll go to the drugstore now. Give you some time to think. But two things to consider. Number one, this is a one-shot offer. When I get to Italy, I will be calling a service. I have to have a nanny. I would prefer someone I know, and someone who seems to know what Darcy needs. You fit both categories. Number two, how long do you think it's going to be before the press gets wind of this?" He motioned around her empty condo.

"The press?"

"The FBI doesn't march up and down a street in the Upper East Side without the media noticing."

"I'm not worried. I'm not the one who stole from my clients."

He snorted a laugh. "That might be the reporters' angle. Innocent daughter of embezzler loses her home. They're guessing you're upset. They're guessing you might know stuff about your mom that will make a juicy story."

"I didn't even see my mom when she offered me this place. I got the keys from the doorman. We don't have brunch or girls' night or wine Wednesday. I know nothing about her. I was an available body to live in an investment property.

If her secretary had been without somewhere to live, she would have just as easily offered it to her."

"Sounds like an interesting story to me."

She squeezed her eyes shut. Her nonexistent relationship with her mother added to her mom's embezzling did make one of those melodramatic made-for-TV stories.

Damn it. She hated being thought of as pathetic.

Wyatt said, "I think you need to get out of the city. Two weeks is long enough for the story to die down and for you to prep yourself for what you're going to say if they do find you." His head tilted. "And they will."

Damn it! They *would* find her if she moved to any one of the five boroughs…or her father's house. Sheesh, of course, they would look for her at her father's house! And that was where she had planned to stay until she found another job and a rundown apartment she could share with roommates.

"Plus, if you come to work for me, you'll be under the umbrella of my legal team and PR team. They can say no comment for you a million times. Protect you."

She froze. That sounded a lot better than dodging reporters and hiding in whatever shabby apartment she could find—that is, if she didn't get fired from her current job. Actually, it didn't matter if she got fired. Her waitressing job in a diner didn't pay enough for expenses, let alone food. As of today, she needed a new, full-time job. But if her name hit the papers, she might have trouble finding someone who would hire her. Especially as a waitress in a classy restaurant where she could earn decent tips.

"The PR department can help you control the narrative. Better yet, they can help you create one." He frowned, running his hand over his beard as he thought. "You need a story. Even if we stick solidly with the truth, it must be written in such a way that it comes out correctly. You know. The PR department creates a paragraph or two of information that doesn't leave room for questions. Something you can say to everybody who approaches you."

Her brain homed in on that. She could see herself with her head high and her shoulders back, easily reciting a prewritten line or two that got her away from reporters and explained things to prospective employers when she went for job interviews.

"Keep talking."

"Nope. That's all I have to say." He headed for the door. "I'm leaving for the drugstore. The decision is up to you. The limo will be out front at three. Have Pete bring your bags down. If you're not there, I'll call a nanny service in Italy. It doesn't matter either way to me. But I think you'd make a good caregiver for Darcy—better than a stranger—and as I said, I'll pay you."

Sophie watched him leave, then with the FBI almost done taking all the things her mother had bought, all the furniture, all the lamps, all the rugs, she walked back to her bedroom to pack her clothes.

Though the idea of a legal team and a prewritten statement by professionals tempted her, she couldn't go to Italy with an ex who had seriously broken her heart—

Could she?

No. That was—

Was what?

She had no idea. She was homeless and would be the target of God knew what until the story died down.

The reality of her situation rolled over her. The FBI seemed to realize she didn't know anything, but that could make her story more interesting to the media. She'd be the abandoned daughter. The child her mom left and didn't even call to see how her life was going. She was literally the perfect avenue for the press to make her mother's arrest juicy and titillating. Stealing from clients was bad. Not even talking to your child? That made Erica Wojack heartless.

Sophie stretched away from the suitcase she was packing. She really did need a professional to word her story.

She took a breath, thought about what she was signing up for in Italy if she became Darcy's temporary nanny. She'd be rescuing poor Darcy from having to go to meetings. She'd dated Wyatt White long enough to know that his negotiation sessions lasted ten or twelve hours a day. That poor baby would be stuck in the carrier on his chest for hours on end.

No child should have to endure that.

But those long meetings also meant that she'd barely see him. Add that to the fact that they'd broken up three years ago and she was over him. He'd hurt her, and she was smarter than to make the same mistake twice.

She did need time to think all this through. Especially how she would handle it in public.

She might not be going to jail, but the internet was forever. How she behaved would end up on YouTube and whatever new platform was being invented. Future employers would see her either calm and composed or frazzled—or angry. Part of her really wanted to be angry. When she was little more than a baby, her mom had left her with her dad, a blue-collar worker who just made ends meet. She'd had no chance at school until her mom plucked her out of her dad's apartment in Queens and gave her a shot at fixing her life.

Only to have it all snatched away—not because her mom had sold the condo—because her mom had *embezzled from clients*. If she thought about it too long, her head wanted to explode. And she did not want that on the six o'clock news…or the internet.

Wyatt was right. She needed a story and it had to be solid and well-written enough that it wouldn't make her look pathetic or like a hot-head.

She also needed two weeks out of New York, a break before she had to face the repercussions of the crimes of a mother she didn't even know.

She'd be crazy not to take him up on his offer.

CHAPTER TWO

SOPHIE CAME OUT of the Montgomery, hiding from reporters in sunglasses and a big hat. She took a deep breath and headed toward Wyatt's limo, carrying an overnight bag and a cosmetic case, and wheeling a suitcase behind her. Pete followed her with three more cases.

Tall, slender Wyatt straightened away from the back fender of his limo. He still wore his black suit and tie, and dark-haired Darcy still slept in the baby carrier on his chest. His striking blue eyes homing in on her things, he frowned. "That's a lot of stuff for two weeks."

"That's everything I own." She looked at what was left of her life. "I have nowhere to go. Nowhere to store any of it."

Wyatt grimaced. "Sorry. I forgot. How many bags you have doesn't matter. We're taking the company's private jet. You could bring a washer and dryer and we'd have plenty of room."

She knew he was trying to cheer her up, but

she didn't feel like laughing. It was one thing to totally restart her life in Queens. She would have sucked it up and found a new job and an apartment and roommates. But face the press? Answer questions about the mother with whom she had no contact? Tell the world that she was the daughter of a thief and a liar? Not be able to find a fulltime job because of all the publicity?

She needed help figuring out a response for reporters or at least some time out of town while the excitement of her mom being arrested died down.

Pete began to stow her suitcases and Wyatt pointed at Darcy, asleep in the carrier on his chest. "I'll get her settled. Join us when you're done." He walked to the passenger's section of the limo and climbed inside, closing the door behind him.

Sophie waited for Pete to finish with her luggage. When he closed the trunk lid, she offered him a tip, but he refused it. "I'm going to miss you, kid."

The sense of permanence of what was happening rattled through her. She might never see Pete again. Never have a reason to walk on this street. She'd probably never have a reason to come to this part of the city.

Her heart stuttered as she looked at the beautiful building she'd called home for three years.

Still, she mustered a smile for Pete. "I'll miss you, too."

He headed into the Montgomery and Sophie slid into the backseat beside Wyatt.

"I'm glad you decided to come with us."

"Yeah, well, you always were able to see all the angles of a problem. I was so gobsmacked this morning, it didn't occur to me that the press would want to interview me, let alone turn this into a spectacle. I'm amazed they weren't waiting on the street for me."

"I paid Pete to tell them that you'd sneaked out using the service entry and were long gone."

She glanced at him, surprised he'd done that, though she wasn't sure why. He *did* think of everything. Always.

He smiled and a bubbly feeling filled her. She was on her way to romantic Italy with the man she'd once been crazy about—

To care for his child.

She gave herself a shake. This was not a pleasure trip. He'd broken her heart. It had taken her a year to get over him. She would not forget that.

In the car seat beside him, Darcy stirred. At first, she kind of whined, then she whimpered, then Wyatt slid a pacifier into her mouth.

The strangest realization drifted through her. She knew she was on a mission of mercy, saving Darcy from hours on end at meetings, but she suddenly realized that this little girl had been deserted by her mom the way Sophie had.

"I give her the Binky before she wakes up completely," he explained. "This might help her go back to sleep. By the way, thank you for your advice about teething. Spoke to the pharmacist and bought enough chew toys and numbing agents to keep her happy for two weeks."

Sophie tried to smile but as the limo drove into traffic, it all seemed surreal. She and her ex-boyfriend's baby were kindred spirits of a sort. The man who'd dumped her like a hot potato when he realized she was getting serious, the man who'd told her he'd never marry and forget—absolutely forget—about having kids, had hired her to care for his child.

That stung. How does a man who breaks up with her because he doesn't want to be a dad suddenly become father of the year?

She settled back on the plush limo seat and took two calming breaths, telling herself not to overthink this. If she let herself imagine the possible scenarios for how he'd become so good at caring for Darcy, she'd only feel like he'd lied to her about why he'd broken up with her. And if he'd lied, what was the real reason he didn't want her around anymore?

Had she done something wrong?

Or was there just plain something wrong with *her*?

Best to keep this simple. She knew how to care for a baby. He needed someone to care for his baby. Plus, she would barely see workaholic Wyatt once they got to Italy. That was the important thing to remember. She might have to get through a ride to the airport and then a flight to Italy, but she had a book to read. She could ignore him.

She *had to* ignore him. She couldn't lose herself in those blue eyes or remember how good they were in bed together—

The air in the limo suddenly became thick and heavy. Though there was space between them, her skin tingled from his nearness. She chalked it up to the bizarreness of being beside her ex-boyfriend—being *employed* by her ex-boyfriend—and looked out the window.

But thoughts of Darcy sneaked up on her again. She knew what it was like to be abandoned by the woman who'd brought her into the world. She knew the feelings Darcy would have when she went to preschool and grammar school and even when she graduated college.

Wyatt would have his hands full.

When they arrived at the private airstrip, staff made short order of their luggage as Wyatt jogged through the light rain to the jet's small stairway, with Darcy covered up in the carrier he held. She followed behind with her cosmetic case and overnight bag, feeling like a homeless person—which, technically, she was.

Her breath stalled when she stepped inside the jet. The space looked more like a living room than a plane. Seats were white leather. A wet bar lined the back wall.

Wyatt pointed at a door beyond the bar. "There's a bedroom back there. Once we take off, I'll put Darcy into the crib."

Awestruck and seriously out of her element, she said, "Okay."

He sat and began fastening Darcy into the car seat already attached to the seat beside his. "Your things can go in that overhead bin." He pointed at the space behind the seats but before the bar. "Sit anywhere you like."

She nodded, stored her cases, then sat on one of the plush seats. As the supple leather cradled her back and butt, she almost sighed at the luxury of it.

"Once we're airborne, there's a TV. Flight's long. Seven or so hours." He finished buckling Darcy in and glanced up at her. "Once Darcy's in the crib we can have the television as loud as we want out here. Bedroom's soundproofed. It won't matter."

"No worries." She displayed her book. "I came prepared."

"Okay. Then you won't mind if I watch soccer."

The less contact they had the better. "No. Watch away."

The plane took off. In minutes, the jet hit the right altitude for a smooth ride, and Wyatt took the baby to the back. When he returned, he plopped down on his seat and pulled a remote from the armrest. "She's in a deep sleep. I don't think I've ever seen her this out of it."

"That's good."

"Well, we'll see if it's good when we get to Italy. Seven-hour flight. Six-hour time difference means it will be five o'clock in the morning when we arrive. She might want to stay awake and play. She'll get adjusted to the time change, but we won't." He glanced at Sophie as he flicked on the TV. "Might be best for us to catch a nap on the flight too. I'm sure Signor Bonetti will want to meet with me first thing after we land, and I promised Trace I wouldn't take Darcy to any meetings. So, you'll be the one watching her."

"That's fine. Great." Being his nanny was her purpose for going to Italy with him, but those feelings of being a kindred spirit with Darcy suffused her again.

Wyatt got comfortable in the seat to watch soccer.

Though Sophie told herself to open her book, she covertly studied him.

Memories of their breakup eased into her brain again. He'd been so emphatic about not wanting kids. He'd called marriage and kids traps. He could have changed in the three years they were apart. But could he have changed so much that he could raise a little girl who'd been abandoned? She knew firsthand how difficult it was to grow up knowing your mother hadn't wanted you.

Unless Wyatt hadn't really broken up with her because of the whole marriage and kids issue? Had it been a convenient excuse and the real reason he'd broken up with her was actually something related to *her*? Maybe telling her he didn't want kids was a breakup line? Maybe the actual reason he didn't want her would have made things complicated? Not the easy cutting of ties they'd had when he told her they wanted two different things out of life, which was something she couldn't argue.

Confusion washed over her only to be booted aside by suspicion that he'd lied to her…

She shook her head to dislodge all those thoughts, reminding herself she was overthinking again. She'd lost her condo that day. Her mom was going to jail. She'd taken a job as a nanny. That was enough to stress about. She did not need to add to her list of worries.

She read for a bit, then the motion of the plane made her sleepy. She kept reading but her eyelids drooped.

Wyatt glanced over and saw Sophie was nodding off. He plugged in earbuds to send the noise of the soccer game directly to his ears. He watched to the end, then he fell asleep too. Sophie shook him when they were about to land, telling him the copilot had told her to wake him.

Dazed, he raced back to get Darcy who was cooing in her crib—with a dry diaper, meaning Sophie had been attending to her. He prepared himself and Darcy for landing and before long, he, Darcy and Sophie were in another limo, leaving the private airstrip and heading to the house Signor Bonetti had rented for him near the small town of Bellagio on Lake Como.

Even in the predawn, half-light of the twenty-minute drive, Wyatt could see lush greenery everywhere. The enormous lake seemed to cradle the small towns that rimmed it in a loving hand.

As the limo navigated the circular drive to their home for the next two weeks, Sophie gasped. "It's a mansion!"

The limo stopped by the well-lit front door,

and he glanced at the spectacular three-story pale stucco house. "It's a villa."

The driver exited the limo, as two young men ran out of the house and headed for the trunk to get the luggage.

Sophie turned to Wyatt, one eyebrow cocked. "You hired staff?"

"Signor Bonetti said the villa came with staff."

She frowned, but he laughed. "Are *you* going to cook and clean for two weeks?"

She peered out the car window at the enormous building again. "I doubt I could clean the whole thing in two weeks, let alone cook, clean and care for a baby. What a place!"

Wyatt sniffed. "It's a negotiating tactic. Signor Bonetti wants me to see he has plenty of money and doesn't need anything from Three Musketeers Holdings."

Climbing out of the limo, still ogling the gorgeous house on the enormous estate, Sophie said, "Really?"

"Yes." He shook his head. "This guy knows every trick I know. It is going to be a blast wrestling his company away from him."

Sophie faced him. "Fighting is going to be fun?"

"First, it's negotiating. Not fighting." He lifted Darcy's carrier out of the limo. "Second, if it's not fun, I don't do it."

"Yeah. Right. No kidding."

She headed up the walk, shaking her head and he followed her. He almost blamed her snarkiness on lack of sleep then he realized that since she was one of the things he'd walked away from, she probably thought she was one also of the things he considered not fun.

Which wasn't true at all. She was the most fun person he'd ever met. But their life goals weren't the same. And he didn't want to have to explain why he didn't trust marriage, or family, or commitment. He didn't want to admit that his dad cheated, and his mom tolerated it. That their marriage was a sham. A front. His dad really hadn't committed to his mom when he took his vows and ultimately his mom didn't care as long as she kept her place in high society.

Worse, he didn't want to admit that his parents had used him as a trinket, the brilliant boy they trotted out to impress friends.

As he carried Darcy up the walk, all that reasoning coupled with Sophie's odd reaction to his comment about fun, and he stopped dead in his tracks.

He'd told her he didn't want kids, yet here he was with a baby.

He held back a groan. No wonder she was behaving oddly.

He'd told her one thing and done another.

Still, they weren't dating. He'd hired her to be a nanny. He didn't have to explain anything to her. In fact, it might actually be easier to let the oddness between them take root. That way they wouldn't have to worry about their attraction finding footing in the beautiful Italian countryside.

His brow wrinkled. *He wasn't worried about that...was he?*

No. They'd been apart three years. There would be no rekindling their romance. He rolled his eyes at the stupidity of that even crossing his mind.

In the big foyer with a two-story ceiling, an ornate chandelier and marble floors, Sophie reached for Darcy's carrier. "I found bottles in the little fridge in the plane's bedroom and fed her before you woke up."

He didn't let go of the handle. "Then she should be good for a while."

"Okay, but she could probably use a change of clothes. Maybe even a sponge bath," she said, attempting to grab the carrier again. "Since it's morning here. It wouldn't hurt to start her on the schedule she'll be following for the next two weeks."

He took a step back. "I'll do it."

She took a step forward, once again trying to finagle the baby away from him. "You go call Signor Bonetti."

He tugged Darcy back out of her hands. "He'll call me."

She put her fists on her hips. "You do realize you have to leave this child with me sometime, right? Otherwise, I'm not a nanny. I'm somebody who attached herself to your trip."

An uneasy feeling wove through him. He wanted to raise Darcy totally differently than how he was raised. He did not want her left with nannies—strangers—the way he had been. Still, this was Sophie, a woman he'd dated for six months, a woman he knew, a person he liked. *A person he'd hired.*

Plus, his partners were right. He couldn't care for her while he and Bonetti conducted business. Having someone he knew as Darcy's nanny, even if it was only for two weeks, was a good way to start acclimating himself to leaving her when they returned to Manhattan.

He handed the baby carrier to Sophie.

She sized him up as she took the handle, as if she was trying to figure him out. He thought of her probable confusion over him even having a child, let alone being an overprotective father and the need to explain himself tiptoed through him again.

Luckily, his phone rang. Seeing it was Signor Bonetti, he answered it as he walked back down the hall, looking for a quiet room or an office.

"Buongiorno!"

"Buongiorno, Signor Bonetti."

"We meet this morning?"

"Sure. I slept on the plane. Name a time."

They set a meeting for nine o'clock, and after they hung up, Wyatt asked a maid for the location of the nursery. Expecting her to speak Italian, he was surprised when she spoke perfect English. After she gave him the location of the nursery, she told him about the cook and housekeepers, as well as the gardener and driver.

As the maid walked away, Wyatt shook his head. Signor Bonetti was showing him how smart he was and his level of attention to detail. This guy was going to be holy terror when it came to coming to an agreement on the sale of his shipping company.

He climbed the stairs and walked back the hall to the last door on the right. Opening it, he saw Sophie with Darcy and he froze.

"Do you like the sundress?" she was saying to Darcy. "You've been in that pajama thing all night. I figured you were probably glad to get out of it."

Darcy cooed and gooed, and Wyatt's heart swelled. He'd never really seen her behave that way with any of her nannies. Though it was far-fetched to think the baby already liked girl talk, or even knew what girl talk was, she seemed to like Sophie.

"At this point, I know you're not watching your figure. So when your daddy's off the phone we'll ask him what you can eat for breakfast."

"She likes peaches."

Sophie turned away from the changing table with a smile. "I like peaches too." She faced Darcy again. "Breakfast will be yummy."

"I sometimes mix it in with cereal."

"Nice." She winked at Darcy. "Some stable carbs for a morning of playing."

The baby laughed.

Darcy had never laughed for any of the other nannies. But she hadn't liked the other nannies. So maybe there had been a good reason for Wyatt to fire them? It wasn't him who'd made the choice. It had been Darcy.

Satisfied with that reasoning, he walked farther into the simple ivory nursery with yellow, pink and blue accents in blankets, pillows and curtains that billowed in the sweet Italian breeze coming in through an open window.

"We should probably scout out the kitchen, see if there's a maid or cook or a maid who cooks."

Sophie lifted Darcy from the changing table and put her on her hip. "Lead the way."

Wyatt held out his hands. "I can take her."

"And put her in that carrier on your chest again? Let's give her a break."

"The carrier is perfectly comfortable."

"Yeah. But variety is the spice of life."

Darcy giggled up at her.

Wyatt's heart swelled again. All his qualms about leaving Darcy while he worked disappeared.

"You are the cutest little thing," Sophie cooed to his baby girl as she headed for the door. "You've got your daddy's blue eyes and black hair and I've gotta tell you, your dad's going to go nuts over all the boys who will be chasing after you when you hit sixteen."

Not sure if he should be happy or confused that his child and his ex-girlfriend had bonded so easily, he followed her out of the room. "I won't go nuts. I understand life."

Sophie sniffed a laugh. "Right."

"I know she's going to want to date."

She stopped and faced him. "Wyatt, I know I brought it up, but don't let yourself think about this now. You will make yourself crazy. Enjoy her as a baby and a little girl. Save the worry about her dating for her teen years."

He considered that, more interested in Darcy's good mood right now than her behavior sixteen years from now.

Hoping against hope Darcy's easy acquiescence wasn't a fluke, but also needing to understand it before he trusted it, he said, "She's not crying."

Darcy babbled happily.

Sophie dropped a quick kiss on her cheek. "She's a cutie pie. Aren't you, sweetie?"

The baby laughed.

Wyatt still wasn't convinced. What if she was happy now, but started sobbing when he left?

"She hasn't liked any of her nannies. Cried for every one of them. And not one of them could get her to stop."

"Were you in the room when they were getting to know each other?"

"Yes. I'd hold Darcy to make sure she was calm and happy and could see the nanny in a positive light, hear her voice, get accustomed to her. Then when I thought she was ready I'd shift her over to the nanny and she'd cry every time." He stopped to glance at Sophie. Her pretty face, soft eyes and smiling mouth. "Your smile makes me want to smile back. Maybe that has something to do with it?"

Sophie shifted away, heading down the stairs. "I think it has more to do with the fact that you weren't in the room both times I changed her and got to know her." She shrugged. "Out of sight. Out of mind. She didn't think to cry for you to take her because you weren't around."

Damned if that didn't make sense. Good sense.

Sophie said nothing, but when they got to the bottom of the steps, she paused and asked, "Which way?"

There was that smile again. Not merely an indication that Sophie was a happy soul, but a link, a feeling that a person could let their guard down with her. She was so easygoing and happy he'd always felt like he'd known her forever. Even on the day he met her. Simply because she was so welcoming.

The urge to confide in her about Darcy's birth mother rose up, but he squelched it. Talking about Shelly infuriated him. They'd literally had a two-week affair—which she'd initiated—and then she'd disappeared from his life. When he was in a cynical mood, he suspected their affair had been all about her desire to get pregnant. But that thought more than infuriated him. They'd talked about birth control. She'd assured him she handled it. Then a little over a year later she was on his doorstep with a baby, telling him she had gotten a job offer in Dubai she couldn't refuse, and he was going to have to raise Darcy.

What person wouldn't be shellshocked?

It wasn't merely a breach of trust; it was disturbing to discover she could so easily hand over a baby. One minute, she would have kept his child from him forever. The next, she was in his living room, telling him he had to step up. He would have never known he was a father, if she hadn't decided she wanted the career boost more than to be a mom.

Anger inched through him again. He calmed himself the way he always did. With the realization that he loved Darcy and how she came into this world and his life was of no consequence. There was no point in talking about it. No point in remembering how easily Shelly had broken the bond with their beautiful daughter and left her behind. Simple acceptance of Darcy had worked to dispel the anger so he could step into the role he needed to play. He'd stick with that.

"The kitchen's just down that hall." He pointed to the end of the corridor and the oak door leading to another area. "There's a cook. Tell her what you and Darcy want to eat, and she'll make it. I've got to get a shower and make myself presentable for the meeting." He leaned forward to kiss Darcy's cheek. "I'll be home as soon as I can."

"Take your time."

"No. I'll be home when I'm done." Because he wouldn't leave his little girl any longer than he had to. Not just to keep Darcy from the lonely childhood he'd endured, but because Darcy's mother hadn't wanted her.

Though if anyone would understand that it

would be Sophie. But that was actually the problem. He didn't want to create any sort of bond with Sophie. Not even friendship. She needed him. He needed her. When these two weeks were over, they would part ways.

Getting too friendly would make that difficult.

CHAPTER THREE

SOPHIE SPENT AN enjoyable day caring for the baby. The weather was gorgeous with a golden sun that smiled down on them as they lounged by the sparkling pool, while the scent of flowers, rich earth and the sea somehow combined to create an intoxicating aroma that drifted around them. She'd taken Darcy for two walks, one in the morning and one in the afternoon, just looking at gardens and grottos in the incredible green space.

That evening, with Wyatt already gone for eleven hours and showing no indication of returning soon, she tucked Darcy in, thinking Wyatt had been correct. This really was the perfect place for her to clear her head and relax.

As she turned away from the crib, the nursery door opened. Wyatt walked in. Wearing the white shirt and dark suit pants he'd changed into for his meeting, with his tie loosened and the suit coat gone, he had the whole sexy businessman thing going on. Memories of their life together flashed through her head, and she understood why it had taken her so long to get over him. He was handsome, cultured and hardworking. Normal in some ways. Perfect in others. Like when he was being romantic. Nobody kissed like he did.

Her breath stuttered in and fluttered out. Those kinds of memories were why she couldn't get too comfortable on this trip. She knocked them out of her brain.

"She's asleep?"

She nodded as he walked to the crib and glanced down at his little girl.

"This is one of the reasons I didn't want to leave her with a nanny. I make it a point never to look at my watch or phone while I'm with someone, so I don't appear overeager or bored. I had no idea I'd been gone so long."

"She's fine." His devotion to his daughter made her smile, even if she didn't understand it. "And you're fine. Take a few extra minutes in the morning with her. Or, better yet, you be the one to wake up with her tonight when she cries."

He faced her and caught her gaze. "You think I won't?"

She shook her head at his serious tone. "Lighten up, Wyatt. Nothing about you surprises me."

He took a step closer. "Really?"

His nearness brought a rush of heart flutters and gooseflesh. She almost said something sassy, something flirty. But this was the precipice. The right response from her could topple them over the edge into flirting, if only because that was familiar. They'd loved to banter, to be light and silly. And his one word was as much an innocent question as it was an open door.

Did she want to flirt with him?

Did he want her to flirt with him?

In the ten seconds that time stood still, she decided to say nothing. Just in case she'd misinterpreted his encouraging tone, or made something out of nothing, she held back every possible response from silly to sexy simply by stopping her tongue, not letting it form words.

He turned to the crib for one last look at sleeping Darcy. "Since she's fine, why don't we go to the patio for a glass of wine?"

Her chest swelled with longing, but her brain told her joining him for anything was not a good idea. Though three years old, the memories of them together that popped into her brain felt fresh and real. Best not to tempt fate.

"No. I'll pass. Darcy might have settled into our new time zone nicely, but technically we were up before dawn. Despite our naps on the plane, we're still on Manhattan time. I'm exhausted. I'm going to bed."

He eased his gaze over to hers. "There are actually a few things we have to discuss."

Oh, those eyes. Blue like the ocean, but serious and curious. She could always tell his mood by his eyes.

"We haven't talked salary yet. What if you don't like what I'm offering?"

The need to be with him, to be the lovers they'd been three years ago, swept through her, but common sense fought it back. She was susceptible because she was tired. She needed a good night's sleep before she could be alone with him at night in a scented garden with stars shining overhead. She was not here as his old girlfriend, his former lover. She was here as the nanny for his *baby.*

The reminder doused her longing and might have even made her a little mad that life had been so good to him and so dreadful to her. "If I don't like your offer, I guess I'll have to take the next plane back home."

His blue eyes shone with laughter. "So, what you're saying is I should pay you less than the price of a ticket back to the states, so you're forced to stay with me if only for a ride home?"

The urge to say something sassy returned. To walk her fingers up the buttons of his perfect white silk shirt while she gazed in his eyes and knew...absolutely *knew*...he wouldn't be able to resist her.

Every time she'd decided to seduce him, he'd gone from purring like a kitten to growling like a tiger, taking her like a man starving...for *her*. Only her.

The memory of that power was intoxicating.

This was why she'd never even let herself run into him in their building. There was something delicious and spicy between them. Sexual. Possessive. They'd been so close, so perfectly attuned, that the last thing she'd expected was that he'd let her go. Whatever they had, it had wrapped around her heart and soul and tied them up in a pretty red ribbon as a gift for him. She'd thought he felt it too. But he couldn't have.

And she couldn't invite him into her life again, only to be set free when they returned to New York. She had experience with how difficult it was to lose him. She'd be a fool to set herself up for that again.

She turned to the nursery door. "We can discuss salary in the morning." She faced him again. "And make it good. I'm going to need a security deposit on a new place. Not to mention lamps and rugs and bed linens."

She left the nursery and entered her bedroom, her heartbeat like thunder. She hadn't forgotten that odd, possessive feeling, but she hadn't remembered its power. Part of her wanted to sink into the memory of him backing her into a corner and stripping her slowly so he could take what he wanted.

The other part knew that was dangerous ground.

And the biggest reason to stay the hell away from him. No breakfast. No coffee. No drinks after dinner… Hell, no dinner together.

No matter how smart she was, he was still gorgeous and masculine. He was a serious guy who also had a sense of humor. She'd loved him enough to want to marry him and have children. He did not feel that for her. It took a whole year to get over him. It would be foolish to forget that. Even being friends didn't seem like a good idea. She should just get through these two weeks.

The next morning, she woke to sunshine pouring into her window. And no sound from the baby. She pivoted to see the clock. Realizing it was almost nine, she bounced out of bed and raced to the nursery but stopped short of the door. She could hear Wyatt talking to Darcy. Gooing. Cooing. Laughing.

She cracked open the door to see him dressed in suit pants, a white shirt and a print tie, leaning over the changing table as he slid his little girl into a sunsuit. For a few seconds she stood and watched him with the baby he wouldn't have with her, letting the insult of that take root. Tempting as he could be, she needed to be reminded that he was pain in a suit.

Then she walked in.

He glanced over with a smile. "I let you sleep in because you seemed to be tired last night."

She had been tired the night before. Otherwise, she never would have let herself open the door to all those memories. But she hadn't forgotten how overprotective he was with Darcy. It was almost as if he didn't trust her—maybe anyone—with his child.

She could understand him changing his mind about not wanting to have children, but there was something odd about the leap he'd taken from not wanting kids to being the perfect father.

Unless he simply hadn't wanted a family with *her*. That made the most sense. Except that also meant the reason he'd broken up with her had been a lie.

She walked to the baby's table slowly, wondering if she should try to figure all this out or let it go. But his gaze fell to the skimpy tank top she'd slept in with pajama pants, and their infernal attraction arced between them again.

One flick of his eyes and they were right back where they were the night before.

The sermon she'd given herself as she'd

climbed into bed popped into her brain. He'd hurt her worse than anyone ever had. And he'd do it again…if she let him.

She didn't want to go through another year of the pain of getting over him. Given their attraction, she had to be a little smarter about what she said, what she did and how she dressed around him.

She broke the powerful connection of their linked gazes. "If you can keep her another minute or so, I can get dressed for the day."

He returned his attention to Darcy. "Sure. No problem."

She left the room and Wyatt blew his breath out on a sigh. He lifted Darcy off the changing table. "You know, breaking up with Sophie had seemed like such a good idea at the time but I have to admit I more than missed her." He shook his head. "But that's wrong because she deserves better. I really could have screwed up last night. I was tired and she did such a good job with you that I was feeling friendly…and I shouldn't be."

The baby cooed and he laughed. "I know she's great, right? But we want different things. And I don't make the same mistake twice. Plus, this isn't about me. It's about her. Making sure she gets the good relationship she deserves."

Darcy's head tilted as if she was confused.

"I get it. You like me so you think I'm a safe bet for everybody." He kissed the top of her head. "But there's a big difference between being your daddy and being…" He frowned again, then finally said, "Sophie's boyfriend."

The word rattled around in his head. *Boyfriend* conjured up images of football games, proms and movie dates. What he and Sophie had, had been intimate. Sensual. And close. They were as close as any two people could be.

Yet somehow, he'd kept his secrets, avoided telling her about his parents and in general let her see only the best part of his life, refusing to think about his past when they were together, let alone tell her about it.

The nursery door opened again, and he started like a kid caught with his hand in a cookie jar. Sophie walked in dressed for the day in a T-shirt that caressed perfect breasts and shorts that showed off long, tanned legs, an indication that she still studied in the park as she had when they were dating.

His chest tightened and he remembered a hundred things best left forgotten by a man who didn't want to get involved with her again. Her bubbly laugh. Her soft moans when they made love. Her soft body.

He pulled in a breath and said, "I take it you're not going into town."

She took Darcy from his arms. Easily. Naturally. And he let her, confusing himself even more.

"If we do decide to go somewhere today, we can change." She headed for the door. "Right now, I'm going to take this little girl downstairs and have Mrs. P. make her peaches and rice cereal."

His brow puckered. "Who's Mrs. P.?"

She faced him with a grin. "The cook. She makes me anything I want for breakfast, lunch and dinner. If you get a free evening where you're eating dinner here, have her make the mushroom ravioli. I had it yesterday." She closed her eyes and sighed. "It is amazing."

Her closed eyes and the sigh reminded him of a particularly good memory they'd shared in the elaborate shower of the primary bathroom of his penthouse. His breathing stuttered and when he tried to talk nothing came out.

She didn't seem to notice as she turned toward the nursery door again. "You get yourself ready for your meeting with Signor Bonetti and we'll see you when you return this evening."

His attraction to her was beginning to annoy him, particularly since she didn't seem to have the same problem. He crossed his arms on his chest. "What if my meeting isn't for hours from now?"

Once again not seeming to be suffering from the same tumble of memories that he was, she turned and motioned toward his suit pants and white shirt. "You'd be in something comfortable."

Not only was she not reliving some of the more interesting moments of their relationship, but also she really did know him a little better than he let himself believe. He should walk away, but a devil inside him wanted one—just one—hint that she hadn't totally forgotten what they had, and he wasn't letting her get away until he got it.

"I still have to eat. So, you're stuck with me through breakfast."

"No. If I remember your work habits correctly, you always go over your notes before meetings. You go to the study. I'll have Mrs. P. bring in scrambled eggs, bacon and some strong coffee."

With that she left and something hot and insistent brushed through him. No matter if she was right. He didn't like her telling him what to do.

Of course, her remembering that he always went over his notes and even what he liked for breakfast actually could be considered the confirmation that she remembered more of their relationship than she was letting on.

His body reacted with a flurry of need, but he shook his head. What the hell was he doing?

Trying to revive memories that would resurrect feelings that would lead to God knew what?

Was he crazy?

No. He was under a little too much pressure. Too much was riding on this deal. He didn't merely want it. He needed it to cement his place as Manhattan's premiere negotiator. Then there'd be no question in his partners' minds that when they needed him to, he could deliver.

There'd also be no question in his father's mind that Wyatt had surpassed him. Made something more of himself than his father had.

Sophie had to fulfill her job as nanny to Darcy in order that Wyatt could succeed and that's all there was. Their nanny arrangement might have turned out to have certain unexpected difficulties—his attraction to her—but he was a strong man who would overcome them.

All he had to do was remember that this deal pushed him past his dad. Only in his early thirties, he would be worth more than his father and better established than his father could ever hope to be.

Then maybe he could get on with the rest of his life.

But to assure that, he needed to spend a little neutral time with Sophie. First, to get accustomed to being around her so that his brain wouldn't slip into fantasy mode every time she

was in the room with him. Second, to make sure
she really was a good choice for nanny. She was
bossy with him. And she used her knowledge of
him from their past relationship as a way to control their situation.

That ended this morning.

Sophie walked downstairs, toward the kitchen,
still overwhelmed by the house that had been
rented for Wyatt as he negotiated with Signor
Bonetti.

With plastered walls housing paintings that
she recognized as originals by masters, the
downstairs reeked of money...but also class. She
paused on the marble floor of the foyer and spun
around once, making Darcy giggle.

"Oh, you liked that?"

Darcy babbled something that Sophie was
sure was agreement. She laughed and kissed her
cheek, even as Cora, the housekeeper who had
introduced herself the day before, came through
the door, wearing a crisp gray uniform and carrying a clipboard, as if the house had a regular
cleaning schedule that had to be adhered to.

"Good morning, ma'am."

So classy and dignified. "Good morning, Cora."

The forty-something woman disappeared behind a door and Sophie took a deep breath, filled
with awe. Everything about this house was per-

fect. Elegant. Even the servants were friendly while still crisp and respectful.

For a second, she felt like a princess in a castle then Darcy babbled, and she headed to the dining room so she could get the little one her breakfast. But she stopped suddenly as reality hit her.

She wasn't a princess.

She was one of the servants.

And despite the gorgeous accommodations, and nothing to do but play with a happy baby and lie in the sun, she couldn't forget she was hired help too.

She carried Darcy into the formal dining room with a long table and twenty chairs, feeling a little foolish as she slid Darcy into a highchair that had materialized after breakfast the day before. Equal parts of wonderful and overwhelming, having her every need attended to felt like part of that fairytale she seemed to be enjoying in her mind, but she was not here to be pampered. In fact, letting herself get accustomed to this life would cause a culture shock when she returned to New York and had to find an apartment she could afford.

She slid Darcy into the highchair as the door between the dining room and butler's pantry opened. The cook entered. With her dark hair pulled back into a severe bun, she wore the same uniform as Cora, but she stretched the fabric to capacity.

"Good morning, Mrs. P."

"Good morning, Ms. Sanders."

"It's Sophie. I'm an employee just like you."

Mrs. P. chuckled. "What would you and the wee one like for breakfast?"

"Peaches and rice cereal for the baby and fruit for me, please." She straightened away from settling Darcy in the highchair and slid onto the soft velvet seat beside it. "Mr. White is in the office working this morning. I told him I'd have you make scrambled eggs, bacon, dry white toast and some very strong coffee and have it taken to him."

Mrs. P. smiled. "Yes, ma'am."

"Sophie, remember?"

"Yes, ma... Sophie."

When she was gone, Sophie faced Darcy. "This might not be my life, but you know this is your life, right?"

The baby grinned and Sophie could see the beginnings of two little white teeth on the bottom gums.

"Your dad is wealthy and brilliant." She frowned. When they were dating, he'd tried to hide it, but she'd always worried that being brilliant was something of a burden for him. People expected things from him. No. People *depended* on him. Though his partners absolutely did their fair share after a business was added to their conglomerate, when it came time to level up, that onus was squarely on Wyatt's shoulders.

She'd always believed she was his release valve. They rarely talked about work. Though she'd met his partners at fundraisers and galas, any time he wasn't working he avoided discussions of business like the plague. Because Sophie was sure he knew the value of time off, of letting his brain rest, of compartmentalizing things so he didn't burn out.

Mrs. P. returned with rice cereal for Darcy and coffee and fruit for Sophie.

"Thank you."

Mrs. P. put her hands on her ample hips. "You should eat something more than fruit."

Sophie laughed. "Oh, trust me. I will. I haven't decided yet if I want a big fancy pasta lunch or a big fancy pasta dinner. But I'll be eating some big, fancy pasta something today."

Shaking her head, Mrs. P. laughed and headed back to the kitchen.

Sophie picked up the baby spoon and scooped out a portion for Darcy. "Don't pay any attention to my eating habits," she said as she slid the spoon in Darcy's mouth and was rewarded by an "Mmm" and some lip smacking.

"Grown-up women balance their food throughout the day but for the next decade or so you need lots of calories because you are growing."

Darcy grinned.

"That's right. Enjoy it while you can."

Eating her bowl of fruit, Sophie fed Darcy, then took her upstairs so they could retrieve the umbrella stroller. "You and I are going to take a walk around the grounds."

Darcy clapped. After slathering the baby with sunscreen, she carried her and the lightweight stroller to the foyer and through a side corridor to a sunroom that led outside.

Walls of glass allowed the morning sun to envelop the room in a golden hue, as they walked through to a door that led to a stone patio.

They'd been out the day before, but after putting Darcy into the stroller, Sophie still paused to admire the conversation groupings arranged on the various sections of the patio, the pool and the gardens among the greenery.

The joyful sense that she was in the Garden of Eden enveloped her as she pushed the stroller toward a segment of wildflowers arranged around a statue of an angel.

"Wait up!"

She turned to see Wyatt walking behind her and frowned. "Aren't you supposed to be working?"

"You're the nanny. Not my keeper."

He was right. She had to remember that and behave—and speak—accordingly. "Okay."

"Where are you going?"

"Just around the grounds." She pointed at cobblestone paths that slid subtly through the rich green grass. "I pick a trail and Darcy and I travel over to see the gardens and statues." She glanced around. "It's so beautiful. The perfect way for her to get some fresh air and sunshine before she takes her morning nap."

"Make sure she doesn't get too much sun."

She laughed. "I'm not a rookie. If I remember correctly, that's why you hired me."

He didn't laugh with her. "I hired you to be sure she's well cared for."

Any residual good humor in her gut disappeared. That was his second reference to the fact that she was an employee. Not his friend. She understood that they needed to keep things professional, but there was no reason for him to question her. "I'm taking good care of her."

"Did you put sunscreen on her?"

"When I went upstairs for the stroller." She huffed out a sigh. "I might not be a real nanny, but I know how to care for a baby. And what I don't know I'll look up. We're fine."

He said, "Uh-huh," but he didn't appear to be convinced.

She took a second to study him then wondered if all this questioning was because they'd come so close to flirting the night before. A ripple of desire wove through her at the memory, but she shoved it aside. He'd hired her because he was desperate. In those minutes, he'd trusted her. Now, suddenly, he was suspicious. That she couldn't do a good job? Or that she wasn't right for the job? Was he thinking about firing her?

After all, they'd had a fabulous relationship, yet he'd still dumped her. And he might have dumped her with a lie. He'd said he didn't want a relationship or kids. Now he had a child.

The whole situation was confusing. And tiring. Extremely tiring when she had to second-guess everything he did.

And why did she second-guess? Because he was behaving strangely.

She knew Wyatt the lover, but didn't know Wyatt the businessman, or Wyatt the obsessive dad. And she didn't exactly like that guy.

What if coming to Italy with him had been the biggest mistake of her life?

She wheeled the baby toward a group of trees at the far end of the path they were on. "Go to work, Wyatt. We're fine."

CHAPTER FOUR

THINGS HAD NOT gone particularly well with him trying to figure things out with Sophie that morning.

Wyatt stirred cream into his coffee, having refused a glass of wine with lunch. Too many things were jumping around in his head. He was being driven crazy by his feelings about Sophie—which were really his own confusion about his longing to sink into their attraction, when he'd ended their relationship for damned good reason. And after today's nonnegotiating session with Bonetti, he now had an odd sense that the old man really didn't want to sell his company.

No. It wasn't an odd sense. Bonetti was beyond procrastinating and foot dragging. He diverted the conversations enough that morning and the day before that he hadn't said two words about his business.

"Your mind wanders. Do you not like lunch?"

They'd eaten at a small outdoor café. Twenty feet beyond their table a fence guided tourists along a path virtually on top of Lake Como. The place was littered with colorful flowers and smelled like heaven. Scents of pasta and sauces mixed with baked goods and greenery. And the ravioli he'd chosen had melted on his tongue.

"I love it." The intense look on Bonetti's face urged him on, but he had nothing more to say about his food. He wanted to discuss the man's company, not lunch. "I'm just thinking about—"

What? If he said he was thinking about financing, Bonetti would jump to the conclusion he was worried about money. If he asked a direct question about his business, Bonetti would deflect.

Suddenly, it all seemed pointless.

Which really confused him. Normally, he loved difficult negotiations.

He motioned for the waitress to come to their table. "You know, I'm actually leaving my child with a new nanny, and that's distracting me. I think I'll go home and make sure everything is okay."

Deflect? Change the subject? Refuse to talk?

Wyatt could do all those too. If the man didn't want to sell his company, turning the tables might flush him out.

He gave the waitress one of his credit cards and rose. "We'll pick this up tomorrow."

The look on short, bald Bonetti's face was priceless. His eyes had widened. His mouth hung open slightly.

Wyatt walked away.

On the drive back to the villa, he wasn't sure if he'd let Bonetti get away with far too much because he was worried about Darcy or concerned about his attraction to Sophie, but a day with his baby and her nanny might cure both. He might not want Sophie bossing him around, but he did want her to take good care of the baby. An afternoon with them could show her that firsthand. Plus, time with her, getting accustomed to being around her again, would probably get rid of the infernal attraction.

Then, when he was satisfied both things were handled, Bonetti had better look out. He was tired of the old man calling the shots and stringing him along.

He drove the villa's sports car onto the winding driveway to the front door, parked and jogged inside. "Sophie!"

One of the housekeepers appeared in the foyer. "She and the baby are outside, Mr. White. In the pool, actually."

He nodded once. "Thank you." Yanking off his tie, he headed upstairs. He changed out of the suit, into swimming trunks and headed to the big sunroom, then the patio, then the pool.

"Hey."

Gliding the giggling baby through the water, Sophie looked up. "Hey."

She wore a pink bikini top that showed off her ample cleavage. As longing swished through him, Wyatt told himself to get used to it. That's why he was here. Outside. *With her.* He had to get accustomed to their blasted attraction, so it would have no power over him.

Her brow wrinkled when she squinted against the sun. "Thought you were with Bonetti all day today?"

"I was supposed to be." He glanced around at the beautiful grounds, surrounded by trees. An opening caused his gaze to stop, and he peered through. "Are there tennis courts back there?"

Sophie laughed. "Yes. There's also a field with soccer goals. When Darcy gets older, you'll have to rent this place again so she can take advantage of all the stuff she's too young to appreciate now."

With one final glance around the beautiful grounds, Wyatt kicked off his flipflops and sat on the edge of the pool, dangling his feet in the warm water. He wasn't sure if it was being away from Bonetti, seeing how happy Darcy and Sophie were or the general peacefulness of the isolated grounds, but suddenly he felt foolish, ridiculous, for believing he was powerless against

an attraction to a former lover and for worryin
about Darcy when it was clear she was happ
with Sophie.

He took a breath and blew it out slowly.

Sophie peered at him. "What's up?"

"Nothing. I just couldn't handle two mor
minutes with Signor Bonetti."

"Are you sure? 'Cause it sort of feels like yo
might be checking up on us."

He moved his feet through the water. Check
ing up on them might not have been his primar
purpose but it had been one of three. Still, the
were fine, and he had lost patience with Bonet
more than he'd worried about Darcy.

"No. I'm not checking up on you."

Her face changed. The questioning loo
changed to humor. "Yes, you are!"

"All right. A little." He didn't want to adm
that he had odd feelings around her. The attrac
tion was one thing. It was natural that memorie
of their good times would pop into his head. H
believed he could end that with enough interac
tion that the memories would stop. His not trus
ing her with the baby dripped of paranoia. H
could see Darcy liked Sophie. He could also se
she was good with the baby.

*So why did this odd feeling about her and th
baby persist?*

He couldn't dislike that his baby was happ

with someone other than him. Not when it served his purposes.

"Truth be told, I used my needing to make sure everything was okay with you and Darcy to get away from Bonetti. He's making me nuts."

Sophie lifted Darcy to her hip then waded farther into the water where it was deeper. Darcy let out a squeal of delight. "Why?"

"Why?" He gaped at her. His nerve endings shot to high alert seeing Darcy in water that would be way over her head if Sophie dropped her, even as complete disgust with Bonetti sent his impatience into the stratosphere. "The man doesn't want to talk business. We've talked soccer. We've talked about Italy. We drink wine. We eat. His kids arrived this morning and sized me up. But we have yet to discuss his shipping company."

"It's only been a day and a half."

Annoyance rippling along his skin, Wyatt slid into the water. "I've negotiated for bigger businesses in a day and a half."

"You've also spent weeks letting a perspective buyer dangle hoping to get the price up for one of your businesses. Was it the holding company for grocery stores?"

He sighed. "Yes. But that deal made me and my two partners billionaires."

"Ah."

He frowned. "Are you saying I'm getting back what I give?"

She feigned innocence. "Me? Why I'm just a simple college girl."

He blew his breath out in disgust. "Right. You're one of the smartest people I know."

She laughed and shook her head. "Because I can keep up with you?"

"Well, yeah. Not everyone can." He frowned again, as memories flitted through his brain. He had always enjoyed talking to her. They didn't discuss his business often, but it hadn't totally been off the table. Neither had politics, religion, art. All things he could bring up to avoid talking about himself, especially his past.

"Anyway, since I'm home I should spend time with Darcy." Walking in the waist deep water toward Sophie, he pointed at the happy baby in her arms. "We'll chill out, and I'll get my bearings back. So that if Bonetti calls to get together tomorrow, I'll be ready."

She passed Darcy to him. "Okay."

He took the baby, then watched Sophie head for the pool steps. "Where are you going?"

"Out. You said you wanted to spend time with the baby."

She climbed the first two steps of the ladder, exposing her little pink bikini bottom and long slim legs. His pulse scrambled and his breath stuttered, reminding him that he hadn't merely come home to avoid Bonetti and see Darcy. He had to get rid of this unwanted attraction. And he'd decided the only way to do that was through spending enough time together that she stopped being a novelty in his life.

"I sort of thought we'd enjoy the day together. The three of us."

She paused and faced him. "Are we back to you not trusting me?"

He winced. What else could the odd feeling he had around her be? "You've only been her nanny two days."

"Yes, but I took care of her *myself* yesterday and this morning. And when you surprised us by coming home early, you found us in the pool, laughing. She's fine. *We're* happy. Actually, we're having fun. It's very nice here."

He sighed. "I know."

She slid back into the water and leaned against the pool wall. "So what's really going on with you?"

He said nothing.

Resting against the pool, she studied him. "You want to know what I remember the most about our relationship?"

Oh, Lord. He wasn't sure if did. If she started talking about their sex life, his libido would not be able to handle it.

When he didn't answer, she said, "It was that you were intense."

He laughed with relief. That he could address. "I buy and sell billion-dollar companies. The fates of thousands of people rest in my hands. I think I'm allowed to be intense."

"Okay. I'll give you that. But I'm talking about being intense about your secrets."

His chest froze. "My secrets?"

"We dated six months. I never met your parents. You rarely talked about yourself. We went to basketball games, out to dinner, fundraisers, gallery openings. We talked about what was happening in the moment, but not really about anything personal. It was like I knew you very well but didn't know you at all. And now, here I am, nanny for your little girl and it's clear there's an issue. Since I've never done anything wrong, never given you a reason to mistrust me with her, I have to assume one of two things. First, something happened in your past to make you so suspicious of people." She caught his gaze. "Or, like you're doing with Signor Bonetti, you're looking for yourself in other people so you can strike first before they manipulate you or cheat you or steal from you."

For a few seconds, he only breathed, so taken aback by her observations that his brain stalled. "Are you telling me I'm a bad person who expects people to do bad things because I do bad things?"

She shrugged. "I don't know. Maybe."

All his beliefs about their relationship flipped on their side. He'd thought she adored him. Only saw the good in him. Wouldn't have believed he had faults. He almost couldn't fathom that she had such negative opinion of him.

The need to defend himself could not be squelched. "That's not it at all."

"So, you're a good guy?"

He always thought he was. Wasn't he?

Sheesh. Now she had him doubting himself.

He straightened up, yanking Darcy higher on his hip. He *was* a good guy. He was fair to his employees, loved his partners like brothers, took in his daughter when her mother abandoned her.

"I *am* a good guy."

"Okay."

Her halfhearted agreement caused the need to defend himself to swell again. Especially when he began seeing their breakup though her eyes. He'd hurt her. Then he'd avoided her. Or maybe they'd avoided each other. He'd done it for her. But what if she didn't see it that way? What if she saw his silences, his unwillingness to discuss his family, as secret-keeping? And mistrust—

Of her.

Worse, she clearly saw his negotiating tactics as heavy handed.

And what if believing wrong things about him, about his motives, about how he'd felt about her had caused her even more pain?

Enough pain that she hated him?

Was that why she was so standoffish with him now? Why she hadn't jumped at the chance to get out of Manhattan but had to think about it?

Because she didn't like him?

He couldn't stand the idea that she didn't like him, that she'd gotten everything wrong because she'd judged him on the secrets he kept, not the great time they'd had together.

He had to fix that.

"Something bad did happen to cause me to be careful with people."

She peered across the shimmering blue water at him. "Had to be pretty bad if you never got beyond it."

"I got beyond it, but it was serious enough that I realize it formed a lot of my opinions and behaviors."

She studied him. "I'm going to need a little more context."

He took a breath, then another. It wasn't like his family life was a secret. Most of Manhattan knew. "My dad cheated on my mother."

Her head tilted, as if she didn't understand what that had to do with anything.

"I caught him."

Her eyes widened. "Yikes!"

The intimation that he'd caught his father in a compromising position almost made him laugh. "No. I didn't *catch* him the way you're thinking. They were at lunch." He floated Darcy through the water, avoiding Sophie's questioning gaze, as he tried to figure out how to explain this in such a way that it shed the right light on his behavior and raised her opinion of him.

"My parents had this 'perfect life' thing going on. My dad was successful. My mom was a pillar of society. I caught my dad having lunch with a woman at a pier. They were in a corner, kissing. It was an accident that I was there. A combination of skipping school and knowing a kid who had access to his dad's boat. In my fourteen-year-old enthusiasm, I confronted him. He left the woman and all but dragged me to his car. He didn't say a damned word for the two hours it took us to get home, but when we got there, he told my mom what had happened.

"They sent me to my room and had a fight, but the next day it was like nothing had happened. Eventually, my mom explained that she and my father decided to reconcile. I thought it was good news. But I caught my dad again and again and again because now he didn't have to hide who he was."

Sophie studied him. "And that makes you distrust everyone?"

"No." He shook his head. "Well, that's part of it. My parents sent me to the best school, and I was a star. But when I wasn't, there were consequences."

Her expression turned horrified. "They beat you?"

"No. They gave me sermons about who I was and what was expected of me and then they'd fly off to Europe or Japan and leave me with a nanny. I never felt like a person. I always felt like a commodity. And no one knew. Everyone saw us as this perfect family which we weren't. But, boy, my parents could pull off the lie. Hug me in front of their friends. Brag, as if they adored me. Not tell anyone how many times I was sent to bed without supper if I got an A minus. And certainly never let on that the only time I was shown any affection was when it benefitted their image."

"That's awful."

"Yes. But in the end, I used it. I realized that life isn't always what it appears to be, and people aren't always their real selves. No one ever screws me over or cheats me. I know the tells. I know how to be careful."

She studied him. "Careful? You're obsessive."

"In a good way."

"Maybe."

"No maybe about it. I live a real life. A genuine life. And so will Darcy."

He could see she was thinking through their breakup and decided to let her draw her own conclusions. The right conclusions this time.

"Look, I don't want you to think I'm crazy. I'm just trying to make sure I get to live the life I want."

"Hmmm. Okay."

She didn't seem convinced. "You think I'm nuts?"

"No. I'm just very middle class, always have been. I've never had to worry about those kinds of things. Your upper-class upbringing was very different than mine. I'm extremely ordinary."

He laughed, thinking she was kidding. Then the expression in her pretty eyes told him she was dead serious. He looked at her with her long blond hair streaming around her and her pink bikini showing off her perfect figure and he knew she wasn't ordinary. Someday, some smart man would snap her up.

It took a second to fight through the jealousy that rattled through him, but only a second. When he broke up with her, he'd accepted that she'd find real love—with the kind of man who deserved her. What astounded him was that she didn't see she was as far from ordinary as any woman could be.

"You're beautiful and smart and you are not ordinary."

She snorted. "Right."

"I *am* right." Damn it. How had she gotten him to not only talk about things he never discussed, but to bring his beliefs about her into the conversation? "That's why you need to finish school. There's a place for you. A purpose. A strong one. You're going to do something important someday."

Sophie listened to his little tirade, knowing the big problem was that he hated people questioning him. But at least she now understood why. His parents punished him if he wasn't perfect.

That's a very difficult way to grow up.

The baby yawned, and Wyatt carried her to the ladder and out of the pool. Assuming he was taking her upstairs for her afternoon nap, Sophie closed her eyes and leaned back against the pool wall again, confused about their conversation.

Wyatt's story explained a lot of why he acted the way he did. But not everything. Lots of people had tough parents and ended up perfectly fine.

There was more to the story. Something he

was holding back. When they were dating, he didn't trust easily, but she'd proven herself to him, and he'd let her into his life, albeit with limitations. Now, when he truly needed her, he had to trust her in a way he couldn't before and that was not coming easy for him.

No wonder he was having trouble.

Except she'd proven herself with Darcy, too.

The door to the sunroom opened and she glanced behind her to see Wyatt striding out, baby monitor in hand.

She hadn't expected him to return but watching him walk toward the pool made her heart stutter. He was gorgeous. Smart. Usually easygoing with her. Only out to enjoy himself. But on this trip, he'd been anything but easygoing.

Of course, now he had a child.

She stopped her thoughts as a realization overwhelmed her. *He had a child.* If the rumors at the Montgomery were correct, the mother of his little girl had simply shown up and handed Darcy over to him.

No wonder he was different. No wonder his mistrust of people had gone from logical to obsessive.

Unexpectedly getting a child could change a person forever.

He presented the baby monitor before he set

it on a colorful round table. "We'll hear her if she cries."

She drifted a little farther down the wall so he wouldn't bump into her as he climbed down the ladder into the pool.

"I want you to know I meant what I said."

"About your parents?"

"About you. You are attractive, but there's more to you. Especially because you are so determined about everything. Once you get into the workforce, you're going to see how quick you are, and that the sky's the limit. For now, you need to finish your degree so you can get a job and start looking for your place."

She smiled. "Well, there's one thing about you that hasn't changed. You still like telling people what to do."

"I'm guiding you."

She laughed. "I can figure this out myself."

"I don't think you can. The situation with your mom is ugly. You will face controversy when you get home. But you can't let that stop you. Hell, our breakup didn't stop you."

"It might have made me more determined."

"Good. Use the negativity of your mom's arrest to push you to prove yourself."

She licked her suddenly dry lips. They'd gone from talking about him to talking about her.

Though she suspected he'd done that on purpose, she didn't miss the message.

No matter that he didn't want her in his life anymore, he truly believed she was going to do something important someday.

Even as the faith he had in her added to her confusion about why he hadn't wanted her in his life permanently, it also gave her a funny feeling in her chest. She hadn't realized how much she needed someone to believe in her. Having him make a point of telling her he did gave her the sense that he was right. She might be broke and homeless, but she only had two semesters to finish to get her degree. The way to make this work might be finding the best job she could while still going to school. She didn't want to live with her dad and stepmom, but it might be possible for two semesters.

But maybe there were other answers? Other ways to get the money she needed for tuition. Other ways to fix this that she hadn't yet had enough time to come up with.

She dove into the water and swam to the edge of the pool and back again. When she returned to the wall by the ladder, he was beside her.

"So, you agree with me?"

"I'm thinking things through."

"Okay. That's part of what these weeks out of Manhattan are about. Getting time to consider all angles. And you know that if there's anything you want to talk about or anything I can do to help you, all you have to do is say the word."

This calm, reasonable guy sounded like the Wyatt she'd dated.

She looked up to find him gazing into her eyes. She guessed he was looking so intently to be sure she was listening to him, but they had always had a connection. Sexual, sure. But today there was more. He genuinely wanted to help her.

Their eyes locked. The magnetic pull she'd experienced when they were dating rose up in her. But this time it wasn't just about physical attraction. It was about his basic goodness. He had a way of wanting everyone to be successful, not just himself. He wanted everybody to be happy. And maybe that's what she'd liked the most about him. He hadn't seen her as a misfit with an absent mom and a dad who'd moved on, going to the university so long after high school she was the oldest person in all of her classes. He just saw her.

Was it any wonder she'd loved him? Deep down he was the strongest, yet kindest person she'd ever met.

And maybe remembering that was more dangerous than their chemistry. The look in his eyes said he wanted to kiss her. He might have even been drawn to kiss her simply out of familiarity. They'd been here before. Kissed a million times.

Memories of missing him, feeling lost, lonely, pummeled her. She absolutely could not go through that again.

She stepped back. "I think I'll check on the baby."

Disappointment flitted through his eyes. "I just put her—" Music suddenly erupted from his cell phone.

"Damn it."

He jumped out of the pool to get it and sighed when he saw the screen. "It's Bonetti."

"Take it." She climbed out of the water and grabbed a big fluffy towel. "I'll check on Darcy and maybe start doing some research online."

For a job. For grants and loans for her last two semesters. It didn't matter which one. She needed to plan her future. She needed something to look forward to, something to hang on to, so she'd stop noticing him, sensing his moods, understanding his new life while getting insight into his old life, feeling that horrible, wonderful attraction that made her long to touch him, to be allowed to be in love with him again.

CHAPTER FIVE

WALKING THE GROUNDS of Signor Bonetti's villa on Thursday morning, listening to the old man jabber on about family and continuity and how he'd assumed his kids would take over his business, Wyatt thought about how much he'd wanted to kiss Sophie—how close he'd come to kissing her. His lips had tingled with the need, but his muscles had quivered with the effort of holding himself back. The urge was that strong.

"This property has been in my family since the Middle Ages."

That brought Wyatt back to the conversation. "Really?"

Bonetti laughed. "You Americans. You think a two-hundred-year-old cupboard is an antique. We count time in centuries."

Not able to argue that, Wyatt nodded. "I wanted to apologize to you for leaving so abruptly at lunch yesterday."

Bonetti waved his hand. "Not a problem. I really called you over to let you know I'd be out of town for two days. I know our negotiations got off to a rocky start. So, I'll spend some time with my grandsons so we can cleanse our palates so to speak, and when I get back, we'll start over. *Si?*"

It made sense to him. As it stood now, Wyatt was losing interest in the shipping company. Which was ridiculous! He needed this purchase. It would be the jewel in the crown of their conglomerate. But when his brain should have been running at full capacity, it was focused on Sophie. Almost kissing her. Wondering why he got so antsy every time she held Darcy.

He saw Bonetti off then returned to the villa. Seeing Sophie and Darcy in the pool, he ate lunch then did some work in the office. But even with all the catching up he had to do he was done around four o'clock.

He paced a bit, knowing they couldn't stay in the house the rest of the afternoon and evening. That was too much time to have to ignore her. He wouldn't be able to do it. Even if he took Darcy outside to explore the grounds, Sophie wouldn't be out of sight, out of mind. He'd proved that when he couldn't stop thinking about kissing her, when he was supposed to be focused on buying a shipping company.

If he didn't do something, he wouldn't just lose the chance to buy Bonetti's business, he'd face the embarrassment of telling his partners he'd failed.

That was unacceptable.

What he needed to do was to go back to his original plan. Bite the bullet and spend enough time with Sophie that he'd get accustomed to being around her, so being with her didn't affect him anymore.

"Sophie?" he called walking out of his office and into the foyer.

She scrambled to the top of the stairs, holding Darcy. "What are you doing home? I thought you were negotiating?"

"I actually came home hours ago. Bonetti wants us to start fresh when he returns from seeing his grandsons. I ate lunch and caught up on a few things."

"Oh." She started down the stairs. When she stepped into the foyer, Darcy reached for him—for the first time since Sophie came into the picture.

His heart swelled with love for the little girl. But the move also reinforced his logic about Sophie. Darcy spent more time with Sophie, so the nanny wasn't a novelty anymore. All he had to do was hang around with her the next two days and he'd be normal around her too.

"How about us doing some sightseeing in town?"

"Or why don't you take Darcy sightseeing yourself, while I get some work done. I need to look up loans and grants for school. And I should also call your PR department to discuss their crafting my statement about my mom and my lack of knowledge of her dealings."

"Right now?"

"Yeah. I need to get started on this. I should at least start investigating grants and loans and then I can call your staff—"

He couldn't believe she was arguing about this. She had to know the rest of their trip would be trouble if they didn't fix their attraction right now.

"Stop. Seriously just stop. Don't you realize how close I came to kissing you yesterday when we were swimming?"

She licked her lips, making him shake his head again. Had she been shocked by that, he would have known it was his predicament to suffer through or solve. But she was having trouble too.

"I know our problem. In the three years since we broke up, we never even ran into each other in our building lobby. Meaning, our automatic reactions to each other are still romantic because our last encounters had been romantic. We need to spend time together as nanny and boss so we can get a new mental identity for ourselves."

She laughed. "Mental identity? That's crazy."

He took a step closer to her, cutting into her personal space. "Is it?"

He'd only crowded her to prove a point, but Sophie's breath stuttered and her pulse raced. The feelings from the pool came tumbling back. Not just the physical desire to touch him but the longing to be in love with him again, to have him love her.

Damn it. He hadn't really loved her. He'd barely told her about himself. All her feelings from three years ago had been one-sided. Her side.

Still, that didn't mean he wasn't right. What if all her reactions around him were simply the result of habit? Having been hurt by him, the last thing she wanted was another romance with him. Yet she couldn't stop the yearning that rose up anytime they were together. Plus, if all her strange reactions around him were only the result of memories, learned behaviors and reactions because they'd never interacted except as lovers, then a little time spent together could get rid of them.

Or it could backfire miserably.

Sometimes life was all about taking a shot. If they didn't at least try to balance out what they were feeling they'd surely end up in bed. But facing the residual attraction head on—bringing it out in the open, not letting it boss them around—might get rid of it.

They were also in gorgeous Italy for two whole weeks. It would be fabulous to spend that time looking around, rather than staying in a house thinking about how attracted they were.

"Okay. You're right. Let me put on something pretty and we can go."

"Sophie?"

Halfway up the stairs she turned to face him. "Yeah?"

"Not something too pretty. We are trying to diminish the attraction."

The silliness of it made her giggle. Though she got his point, her heart lifted. She'd forgotten how much she loved to laugh with him. And how much it pleased her that he believed she was beautiful.

Rather than groan at the memory, she let it and feelings it inspired wash through her. If being around each other was to work to eliminate these feelings, then she had to acknowledge them and replace them with the reality that he might have always thought she was beautiful, but he'd also broken off their relationship.

The hard truth rippled through her and burst the bubbly happy feeling.

Exactly as she wanted—

No, exactly as *they* needed.

Almost an hour later, Wyatt's head tilted when she walked down the stairs to the front foyer. She'd chosen a pink sundress that complemented her blond hair and the light suntan she had from studying in the park and playing in the pool with Darcy.

When she reached the bottom step, he shifted Darcy on his hip and said, "Too pretty."

She laughed, not letting the compliment affect her as it had the first time. "For Italy? Lake Como? Famous for being the home of royalty and movie stars? Frankly, I think I'm underdressed."

He snorted. "Right." Pointing to a corridor off the stairway, he said, "This way to the garage. I found a Range Rover in there when I went looking for a car to drive to Signor Bonetti's. It's more suited for us than the sports car I've been using."

"Signor Bonetti certainly thought of everything."

Pushing open the door that led to a huge garage, Wyatt sighed. "Unfortunately."

"Why is that unfortunate?"

Carrying Darcy, he led her to the black Range Rover. "I told you. He knows all my tricks. That's why his not talking business yet is scaring me. What if there's something I don't know about negotiating that he does?"

"Then you'll use this as an opportunity to learn something new."

One of his eyebrows rose. "Really? That's your take on this?"

"Hey, there's a silver lining in everything. Sometimes it's simply the chance to learn a lesson, but some lessons are pretty damned important."

He rolled his eyes, then opened the door to the backseat and slid Darcy into the car seat that had already been installed.

"You must have gotten downstairs long before I did."

"Let's just say I dressed myself and a baby, installed the car seat and put the umbrella stroller in the trunk in the time it took you to put on that pretty pink dress."

Once again, the fact that he'd noticed pleased her. She shoved the feeling aside and opened the passenger door. "Okay. Point taken."

He slid behind the steering wheel. "I'm not being critical. You're allowed to take time to yourself. Your only breaks are when Darcy's sleeping. There have been days, when I was the only one with her, that I had trouble finding time to go to the bathroom."

Darcy began to babble in the backseat. Wyatt glanced at her in the rearview mirror. "Do you think she's defending herself?"

She turned to look at the baby who was playing with her foot. "Not unless her toes are the jury."

He laughed and started the SUV before he pushed a button to raise the garage door.

"You're getting awfully comfortable with this place."

He backed out onto the cobblestone driveway. "I'm thinking of adding this villa to the purchase of the shipping company to make up for the pain and suffering Bonetti's putting me through."

She snickered. "Have you ever given a perk to one of the buyers of your companies for the pain and suffering *you* put *them* through?"

He gaped at her. "No."

"Okay then."

The drive to Bellagio, a village at the tip of the Y formed by the lakes, was magnificent. With the Alps in the background and greenery all around them, the views took Sophie's breath away.

To her surprise, they parked at the edge of town. "What are we doing?"

"There's not a lot of parking. The streets are narrow and filled with tourists, so it's best to walk."

"You've been here before?"

"I researched."

She laughed. "Of course, you did."

They got out of the SUV, loaded Darcy in a stroller and began the walk along Giuseppe Garibaldi, the main road. The closer they got to town proper, the more tourists milled about the streets filled with shops, restaurants, bakeries and coffee shops. Bright coral, blue and green awnings protected doorways of stucco buildings painted beige or white or yellow. Quaint cobblestone streets guided them along.

"This is amazing."

Wyatt looked around. "It's like a different world."

"It is." She inhaled the sweet air. "I'll bet we could get some really good pastries for breakfast tomorrow."

"And insult Mrs. P.?"

She wrinkled her nose. "Right. We wouldn't want to do that. The woman's a gem. I can't believe I forgot her."

He sniffed a laugh. "It's part of her job to blend in with the house."

She glanced at him. He always behaved so normally it was easy to forget he was wealthy beyond her wildest dreams. But remembering that he'd grown up in the lap of luxury, and bought companies worth more than she'd earn in a lifetime, was another good way of dissolving their attraction. When they'd dated, she'd always believed they were fated to be together, so good for each other it was obvious they belonged together, despite their different stations in life. But losing him had shown her that he didn't look at life the same way she did. And maybe remembering that would be the real way to dispatch the memories that wanted to draw her to him.

They pushed Darcy's stroller along the cobblestone streets until they found a little coffee shop with seating outside. They wheeled her in and sat at a tiny round table. A waiter walked over.

"We've been smelling pastries for our entire walk. Any idea what we're smelling?"

"Could be anything," the waiter said with a grin. "But we have the best *miascia* in Italy. Apples, pears, macaroons and chocolate with just a bit of liquor. There is nothing quite like it."

Wyatt laughed.

The waiter sucked in a breath as if Wyatt's laugh had insulted him. "I'm not bragging."

"Okay. We'll have that and some coffee." He glanced at Sophie. "If that's good with you."

"Sounds great." It did. She hadn't had the big lunch she'd promised herself and it was getting late. Not so late that Darcy needed to be in bed, but late enough that they were officially missing dinner and her stomach was growling.

She inhaled the scent of the sea and all the wonderful pastries with which their *miascia* competed.

As the waiter walked away, Wyatt said, "It must be great to live here."

She glanced around. Even inundated with tourists, the place had a slow, happy pace. She put her elbow on the table and rested her chin on it as she studied him. "You can live anywhere you want. Why not here?"

He bent down and lifted Darcy from her stroller, settling her on his lap. "Business. I like being in Manhattan. It's where the action is."

"Yet here you are working in Italy."

"Courting a pretty tough customer."

"So you say." She frowned then glanced at him again. "You always told me that getting someone's business from them was simply a matter of figuring out what they really wanted and then offering it to them."

"I told you that?"

She shrugged. If bringing back memories of their former relationship was supposed to diminish their attraction, then they needed to talk about their relationship. "You told me a lot of things."

He'd talked about high school and university, old girlfriends and the strong friendships he'd built with Cade and Trace, his first apartment, and the fact that he'd never actually held a job except an internship. All that was interspersed between chats about art and music, New York City, and his travels.

Funny, now that she thought about it, she realized he'd gone to Europe, Australia and Asia with friends, not his parents.

Still, there'd never been a quiet or uncomfortable minute between them. They'd talked in the back of his limo, on snowy walks in Central Park, in fancy restaurants or little burger joints, at Broadway shows during intermission or in his apartment. She could not remember a lull in conversation.

In all those talks, he'd somehow avoided telling her about his parents. Yet, he'd shared that now. When she wasn't actually in his life—except temporarily.

Because it didn't matter?

Because he was putting distance between them?

Explaining why their relationship hadn't worked?

Probably. Just as she knew they had to talk about their old relationship to get rid of it, he was opening up now.

Uncomfortable silence settled over their little table. She'd thought he didn't like his desire to kiss her because he feared getting close again. But what if it really was just a reflex for him? No emotion attached?

Disappointment and foolishness flooded her. She kept forgetting that she'd fallen in love with him, but he hadn't fallen in love with her. He'd dumped her.

Their dessert and coffee arrived. Wyatt returned Darcy to her lightweight stroller and gave her a teether, as the waiter set the order before them.

She peeked at the waiter. "It smells heavenly."

He grinned. "I told you."

He left them and Sophie inhaled deeply, enjoying the full experience. She let Wyatt take the first bite of the *miascia*. He groaned. "Wow."

She took a bite, savoring the flavor that exploded on her tongue. "Wow is right."

"And this is just the first thing we've tried. Can you imagine trying something new every night?"

She could. Except she didn't want to go out with the Wyatt with her now. She wanted to experience it with the Wyatt she'd loved. The guy who hadn't yet broken her heart. The guy who had seemed to love her.

Going out with him in an attempt to break his bad habit of wanting to kiss her was sad and lonely. Now that she was thinking logically of how he'd viewed their relationship, it was easy to see how different he was from the guy she'd dated. Harder maybe. Or perhaps his honesty made him seem different than the guy he had once been?

"I've heard that's what vacations are for."

"True."

She studied him a second. "Have you ever taken a real vacation? Not just gone to some great country to negotiate for someone's company?"

He laughed. "I can see how you'd get that impression. But I love to go to Cade's house in the Florida Keys. I just took Darcy there a few weeks ago."

The fondness in his voice for the child he'd said he didn't want with her saddened her even more. He was perfectly capable of loving Darcy. It was her he wanted to avoid.

She took a breath, keeping the conversation neutral, working as hard as he was now to break his romantic habits about her.

"How long did you stay?"

He shrugged and forked off another piece of dessert. "A couple days."

"Ever stay anywhere for an entire week? Just for entertainment. No work involved."

"I used to. When I was younger. I told you about those trips before I met Cade and Trace in college."

Trips without his parents. No chaperone. No supervision. Almost as if he was trying to escape them. Or they didn't want him around?

"Now, you're more of a workaholic."

"Don't make it sound godawful. I enjoy what I do."

"Except when the other guy is smarter."

He laughed. "Bonetti's not smarter. He's just got something up his sleeve and I don't know what it is. But I'm going back to my old-school philosophy about figuring out what he wants and dangling it in front of him. I'm better at this when I stick with what I know."

She smiled weakly. The young, impulsive guy he was three years ago had been charming and charismatic, but this Wyatt, the guy with substance, suddenly interested her more.

Which was pointless since they were here to get rid of their attraction. "I guess."

They ate their dessert talking about the cobblestone paths, gorgeous houses perched on the hills and the peace of the lake. The ride home was made in darkness and Darcy fell asleep, forcing her and Wyatt to be quiet.

But when they returned to the beautiful villa, emptiness surrounded her. She was beginning to like this new Wyatt. Having him open up to her made her want more. And he wanted nothing to do with her.

"Let me take Darcy to bed."

He held on tightly to the baby. "I'll take her."

Getting Darcy might have softened him in

some respects, but it had also made him vigilant. Determined to love his little girl, even as he shut out everyone else.

"Or we can both take her."

He nodded. "That way we'll have her in bed twice as fast."

She smiled the way a good nanny was supposed to and ignored the tweak in her heart when Wyatt sat on the rocker in the nursery and fed Darcy a bottle before he changed her into one-piece pajamas and kissed her goodnight.

It wasn't amazing that he could be so good to his child. She'd always known that deep down he was kind. What surprised her was that becoming a father seemed to have made him even more alone.

She turned toward her bedroom which was right beside the nursery.

"Goodnight, Sophie."

She stopped and faced him. "Goodnight, Wyatt."

"We did okay tonight?"

She couldn't say. The only thing she'd accomplished was to remember old Wyatt and realize there was more to him now than a big brain and the ability to get what he wanted. Rather than that help her grow accustomed to being with him, to their chemistry, it only seemed to make her miss him more.

CHAPTER SIX

FRIDAY MORNING, when the baby monitor sent the sounds of Darcy crying into his bedroom, Wyatt bounced up in bed. His first thought was of Sophie, but instead of groaning, he congratulated himself on how well their sightseeing went. They'd had short, succinct discussions that weren't stilted. She knew him and that knowledge edged into their conversations. But nothing seemed to tip over into those romantic memories that bedeviled him.

And this was Lake Como! There were hundreds of small towns to visit, hundreds of sights to see. If that wasn't enough to keep them too busy to think about being attracted, the villa owned a boat that was moored in Bellagio. Because of Cade's island, he was very good with handling a boat. They could take Darcy out that afternoon if they wanted.

In his navy pajamas, he stepped into the nursery. "Hey, baby. What's all the crying about?"

Darcy sniffled and rolled over so she could see him. Her short black hair made spikes on the top of her head. Her blue eyes swam with tears.

"Now, now. Mornings aren't that bad." He lifted her out of the crib, his heart swelling with so much love he almost couldn't contain it. "Actually, I like to look at mornings as a new opportunity."

The nursery door opened, and Sophie ambled into the room in a T-shirt and yoga pants, but his brain didn't dart back to a memory. It didn't need to. Seeing her perfect butt cradled in the stretchy pants, he didn't need to recall feelings. New ones sparkled through him.

Well, damn.

Darcy snuggled against him and brought his attention back to where it needed to be. "That's right. Daddy will change your diaper and feed you."

Sophie walked over, her hands open to take the baby. "I'll do it. You get ready for work."

He eased away from her. "No work, remember. Bonetti's out of town, visiting his grandsons." He set the baby on the changing table and took a short breath, trying to decide if they needed more time together or less. If the feelings he had weren't connected to memories, then more time together didn't seem advisable.

Of course, they'd only tried spending time together once. That wasn't enough to know if it had worked or not. Today, he'd make double sure he interacted with Sophie enough that he grew accustomed to her.

Sophie rooted around in a drawer for clean clothes for the baby, which she set on the changing table.

She peeked around him to tickle Darcy's belly. "Good morning." The baby gooed and cooed. "I take it you slept well."

Darcy laughed and made some sounds that weren't words but showed she was grasping for them.

"I slept well too. I think it might have been the walk around town. Made me sleepy."

The baby giggled.

Wyatt didn't know why he was surprised Sophie was so good with Darcy. Not only did she have experience with babies, but she was a likeable person. He'd liked her when they were dating. Obviously, he'd told her a lot more than he typically told people about himself.

Her interactions with Darcy, though, always made him smile. "She loves you."

Sophie tickled Darcy's belly again. "I think she's pretty special too."

Something warm and fuzzy rose in his chest. He got rid of it by telling himself that it was simply love for Darcy and happiness that she liked her nanny that was getting to him.

"She had a good time in the pool yesterday."

Wyatt said, "Yeah. She did. She likes the pool at Cade's. I'm not surprised she likes the pool here."

"It's always good to put her in situations she's comfortable with. That will ease her from her regular routine into this one."

"We don't go to Cade's all the time."

"But swimming or being in the pool is something she's accustomed to."

He shrugged. "Yes. Sort of. I never thought of creating routines for her."

She peeked over his shoulder at the baby again. "Babies love routines. That's what my stepmother said. If they are comfortable, they are happy. Doing familiar things makes them comfortable, so doing familiar things makes them happy."

"That makes sense."

He snapped the last closure on her outfit, and she spit out a string of unrecognizable sounds. Again, seeming like she was trying to make sentences.

Sophie pinched her cheek. "You're so smart."

Darcy said another string of sounds.

Wyatt said, "It seems like she's trying to make sentences."

"I'd say she's mimicking us."

"Interesting."

"It's how babies learn. They watch and mimic and try to figure things out by what they see others around them doing."

Others around them? He was the only one around her most of the time. Meaning, to learn about life, she'd be watching *him*.

His usual fear rippled through him. He had a cheat for a dad and a social climber for a mom. They'd punished him when he hadn't performed. They'd alienated him. Shoved him off on nannies. He hadn't learned a damned thing about parenting from his parents—

He shook his head. He'd always told himself awareness was power. Having seen the miserable way his dad treated his friends, he'd become a better friend. Having seen his mom's love of social climbing he'd not joined the game. He knew he'd be a better parent. He would never punish Darcy for bad grades. He'd never let her feel alone or unwanted.

Still, he was a single guy, someone who used work as play—

"She's *watching* me?"

"Of course! And, right now, she's also watching me."

He said, "That's good." Then realized just how good it was. He was clueless. Sophie knew things.

Maybe instead of hanging around Sophie to get rid of his attraction, he should be paying attention to what she said and did around the baby?

Or better yet, maybe he should be taking notes. Watching what she did. Watching how she treated Darcy. How she cared for Darcy. And then writing everything down so he could refer to it.

He didn't need time to forget his attraction. He needed to learn how to care for his little girl. And he had the perfect teacher in his employ.

Sophie lifted Darcy off the changing table. "You get dressed. I'll go downstairs and tell Mrs. P. the baby's awake and ready to eat. Maybe get her a bottle of water."

He said, "Okay," then frowned at the door after she was gone.

He liked the idea of learning as much as he could while he had Sophie around, but something was happening here. Yes. He needed to learn to care for his child. But for him to open up and ask questions, they would have to become friends. He would have to trust her even more than he trusted her with the baby.

He would have to trust her with his shortcomings, the oddities about him because of being raised by parents who demanded perfection and nannies who shifted every six months or so and only did their jobs.

He'd been raised in the loneliest way possible. It made him different. He did not want Darcy to go through that.

He walked into his room, changed into shorts and a T-shirt and ambled to the dining room where Sophie sat feeding Darcy.

Weirdness tumbled through him. He'd broken off their relationship before they'd gotten too close. Now, suddenly, he was about to expose all his vulnerabilities to her.

He took a seat at the head of the table and Mrs. P. scrambled in. He asked for eggs, toast and bacon. When she was gone, he poured himself a cup of coffee from the pot on a buffet.

"What do you think we should do today?" Coffee in hand, he walked back to his seat. "We have the whole day. We could go out on the boat."

She winced. "I really do want to have an hour or two to look up some options online."

"Did you bring a laptop?"

She nodded. "Yes. It's one of the few things I got to keep because my dad bought it for me for Christmas one year."

"Must be old. Are you sure you don't want to use mine?"

She stiffened. "I'm fine."

"I didn't mean to insult you."

"You didn't."

He surely had. But he supposed he'd be tripping over himself for the next ten days as he tried to get the help he needed and help her in return.

He took a sip of the hot coffee, knowing he had to shift this conversation. "Anyway, what if I gave you two hours, then we headed out on the boat."

"It'll be Darcy's nap time."

"Right."

"I can always do my research tomorrow."

He shook his head. "No. You're eager to get started figuring out your future. You can't do that without investigating a few things like school loans and a new apartment." He peeked over at her. "You might even want to check what's happening with your mom. Or at least see if it's making headlines in the papers or dying down."

She didn't answer for a second. "I'd rather call your PR department."

"You have to wait until afternoon for that. It's in the middle of the night in Manhattan."

"Right."

Her mouth turned down and the light in her usually bright green eyes dimmed. She set her attention on feeding Darcy who looked like she was loving whatever was in the bowl on her high-chair tray.

"What's she having today?"

"Plums and rice cereal."

Darcy smacked her lips as Mrs. P. walked in with Wyatt's breakfast.

"She loves it."

"That she does," Mrs. P. said. "My kids always did."

"Good to know," Wyatt said, expecting Sophie to chime in with her own agreement, but she seemed to be off in the distance.

Mrs. P. scampered out of the dining room and Wyatt glanced at the table where a cup of coffee sat in front of Sophie but no breakfast.

"Aren't you hungry?"

She shook her head. "No. Not really."

He studied her. He hadn't expected that bringing her here would make her troubles disappear. He knew they'd dog her. He knew she'd have some things to face and decisions to make. They'd talked about it almost every day they'd been here. But now that the time had come for her to investigate possibilities for finishing university, she seemed down in the dumps.

"You're okay, though, right?"

"If you're asking if I'm good enough to care for Darcy, the answer will always be yes. I won't let my troubles affect her."

"I'm not worried about that." He knew she'd be responsible. She always was. "Are you upset about your mom or the next few years of your life?"

"It's weird to have a plan and have it snatched away then have to scramble to figure everything out."

He laughed. "Look who you're talking to. I had a plan. A solid one. Then one day an ex, someone I hadn't even thought about in a year just bold as brass walked up to the doorman and demanded to see me. He called me, I went down to the lobby, she showed me Darcy and suggested we talk in my penthouse."

Obviously curious, Sophie perked up.

He hadn't intended to tell her this story, but it seemed appropriate given her new role as his teacher for the remainder of their two weeks in Italy.

"She told me Darcy was mine. Said I could have a DNA test done to prove it. Then said she had a job in Dubai and couldn't take the baby. Her hours would be long, and she wanted to devote herself to this stage of her career."

Sophie gaped at him. "I'm not sure if that's arrogant or heartless."

Seeing her reviving as her interest grew, Wyatt kept going. After all, most of this had been gossip at the Montgomery from the day he got Darcy.

"I couldn't tell, either. She gave me some bull about being thrilled to be pregnant and she didn't need me. She would have raised Darcy alone, but then she got this opportunity and promotions like the one she'd been given didn't come along every day and she wanted it."

"Wow."

"I know, right?" Wyatt said, catching her gaze, feeling like he had something of a kindred spirit in her. "From her story, and the way she hedged about some things, I had the sense that she might have deliberately gotten pregnant, following a whim of wanting to be a mom, and when a chance to further her career came up, she changed her mind."

"My dad said my mom was like that."

He hadn't set out to get her to talk, but he was glad she was opening up. "Selfish?"

She laughed. "No. Scattered. One minute she wanted one thing, the next day she wanted another. No one was more surprised than he was when she started the investment firm and stuck to it." She sniffed. "Now we know why. She was siphoning off money. Probably indulging her whims with other people's wealth." She took a breath, pressed her lips together then caught his gaze. "What's funny is I genuinely believe that she didn't consider anything she did wrong."

"Sophie, she was stealing money."

"Yeah, but I'll bet if I talked to her right now, she'd say she was going to give it back, only borrowing it and everything got blown out of proportion."

Wyatt opened his napkin and set it on his lap. "Unfortunately, that sounds a lot like Shelly. She's got a story for everything. I was going to break it off when she started ghosting me. I thought we were on the same page of realizing we weren't a good match. Seems I was right and wrong."

She nodded and was thoughtful for a few seconds before she said, "I can't call New York. You can't see Bonetti." She shrugged. "Maybe we should go out on the boat this morning?"

His chest filled with relief. He didn't even realize how upset he was for her until she agreed to relaxing a bit. "I think that's a great idea."

Of course, the villa Bonetti had rented for Wyatt had a boat. A simple outboard cruiser moored at a dock a few miles away. Sophie would have shaken her head in disbelief, but nothing surprised her on this trip. In some ways, Lake Como was almost magical. Not only was it breathtaking, but Wyatt had opened up to her again. He'd told her about his parents, then Darcy's mom.

After unloading the car seat from the SUV, Wyatt carried Darcy along the wood planks that took them to the boat and Sophie brought the picnic lunch made by Mrs. P.

"That's a big boat."

"Not really," Wyatt said as he boarded the

cruiser. With Darcy secured on his hip he took the picnic basket from Sophie so she could climb on.

They settled Darcy in a car seat and secured her before Wyatt set out on the water. Leaning against the side of the boat, beside Wyatt who steered the craft, Sophie watched Bellagio grow smaller and smaller the farther out on the water they got. "Wow."

"I know, seeing it from the lake is amazing, isn't it?"

"You have got to buy a property here."

He chuckled and took them out to the center of the water, then stopped the boat. "Let's just get the negotiations with Bonetti done first before we start making decisions like me buying a house here."

"Okay." She'd brought up the subject of him buying property on Lake Como because she was still filled with questions about Darcy's mom. Deciding it wasn't wise to ask those, she kept the conversation on Lake Como. She pointed at the shore. "Look how pretty the houses are."

He drew in an appreciative breath. She could almost see his stress melting away. "Yeah."

Noting how he was relaxing reinforced her decision not to talk about Darcy's mom. They discussed the mountains cradling the lake, Bellagio itself, and even how everything felt different here. Then she let the conversation go. As if carried off on the gentle breeze, her thoughts disappeared, and she turned her face up to the sun.

"Darcy's asleep."

She kept her eyes closed. "It is her nap time."

"Is this good for her?"

"Sure. She's slept in that carrier before. She's comfy. She'll probably wake naturally. Just as she does in her crib."

"Okay."

Wyatt started the boat again, taking them on a leisurely trip around the first arm of the Y of the lake.

A little over an hour later, Darcy fussed and Wyatt stopped the boat, brought Darcy out of her car seat and showed her the shore.

"I hope she remembers it," Wyatt said as he sat beside Sophie on a bench seat.

Relaxing again, she didn't open her eyes. "She won't."

"She won't?"

"She's too young." She opened one eye. "I'm telling you. You're going to have to bring her back here when she's older."

He laughed. "Okay. Whatever."

They ate their lunch, then took a drive along part of the other arm of the Y that formed from the lakes, with Sophie holding Darcy, pointing out things the baby wouldn't remember.

When it was time for Darcy's afternoon nap they decided to return to the villa.

They were quiet on the boat ride back to the dock, quieter still on the drive to the house. Lake Como was the perfect place. Full of peace, it had settled Sophie's mind and she didn't want to disturb the blessed silence in her brain.

She didn't even realize Wyatt had turned off his phone until they pulled the SUV into the garage, and he turned it on again. Bells and pings filled the vehicle.

"Sounds like you've been missed."

He glanced at his phone as Sophie pulled Darcy out of the car seat and snuggled her against her chest.

"Bonetti's home."

"Already?"

"He said he wanted two days. That was yesterday and today. Tomorrow we meet again."

She refused to let disappointment rise. They'd had such a nice day. *He'd* had a nice, calming day. There was no reason to make more of that than what it had been. A break.

"It still feels like he's home early."

Reading something on his phone, Wyatt said, "Because he called today instead of tomorrow morning."

"You think it's a trick?"

He rolled his eyes. "I don't know. He could be

trying to keep me off balance or he could simply be following his own timetable."

"Maybe it's better to think he's inexperienced than to think he's yanking your chain."

He snorted "Probably. Giving him too much credit is throwing me off my game."

"Exactly."

He took Darcy from Sophie's arms. "I'll put her to bed. You can call New York if you want or just use the Internet. If I'm with Bonetti all day tomorrow, you won't get a chance."

She said, "Okay," handing off the baby and heading to her room and her laptop. But she sat staring at the screen. She didn't feel sorry for Wyatt. He had everything. But after hearing him talk and sensing his isolation, she knew he also had nothing. No family who behaved like family. No connection except to two friends he considered to be brothers.

Which was cool. Better than a lot of people had. But there was a loneliness that surrounded him and Darcy.

She couldn't explain it. She thought it best not to try because she didn't want to get involved with him. And he didn't want to get involved with her.

Still, on Saturday, floating Darcy through the pool, she realized that she had only nine or so days as Darcy's nanny and maybe the best use of her time would be to help Wyatt with things he might not think to investigate.

After putting Darcy in a poolside baby swing, she got out her phone and searched *how to teach a baby to swim*.

She learned about vertical twists and assisted free floating and tried both with the baby who giggled with delight.

While Darcy napped, Sophie investigated grants and student loans again, not quite ready to talk to Wyatt's PR department yet. She and Darcy ate dinner, then she put the baby to bed.

It was after nine when Wyatt returned.

Sophie was in the foyer to greet him. "Hey! How'd it go? Darcy and I had a great day. I googled how to teach a baby to swim and found some really neat information. Do you know babies as young as five months can be taught to hold their breath?"

"No. I didn't know."

At the weariness in his voice, she tilted her head, studying him. "He's wearing you out, isn't he?"

"Wearing me out? Wearing me down? Simply a guy who wants to have fun?" He shook his head. "Who knows. The point is, we got nothing done today."

"What did you do?"

"First, we spent the morning talking about the two days we each had off."

Sophie couldn't help it. She laughed. "Sorry."

"Oh, don't be sorry. I'd be laughing if it wasn't happening to me." He headed for the den and walked behind the bar. "After the chitchat, we played eighteen holes of golf."

"Golf?"

He got a glass from the shelves beneath the bar. "Then we had an enormous dinner with the most delicious food I've ever eaten."

"That sounds fun."

"Oh, it was fabulous. Especially since he invited his entire family. We talked about kids and grandkids, vacations, the proper private schools and even university."

"But not his shipping company."

He sighed, setting his glass on the shiny bar. "No."

She shooed him away. "Go sit. I'll pour your bourbon."

"Put some ice in it. If you don't, I'm afraid I'll just start drinking it like shots and that won't be good."

She laughed and he fell to the sofa. "The man is killing me."

She found the bourbon, poured some over ice and handed it to him as she sat beside him. "I don't get it. Can't you just work a discussion of his company in?"

"Oh, I have tried."

The expression on his face made her laugh. "Sorry. Again."

"You think this is funny?"

"I think this might be life telling you that you won't always win."

He gawked at her. "That's unacceptable."

She shrugged. "Either you have to accept his timetable about negotiations, tell him to shove off and leave Lake Como, or somehow get control."

"Yeah. No kidding."

"Come on. Talk to me. Tell me what you're missing. Sometimes saying things out loud can give you the answer."

He took a breath, thinking she was crazy, but also realizing he couldn't go on like this.

"He's so casual, it's difficult to pin him down."

"That's good. Keep talking."

"He's definitely in command at his villa."

"Which might make you feel uncomfortable about pushing him or arguing with him when you're on his turf."

He leaned back, relaxing on the sofa. "Maybe."

"No. No. No maybes. Only state facts."

He frowned at her. Not because she pushed

him but because he suddenly realized that on this trip he'd told her about his parents, told her about Darcy's mom and now she was getting him to talk about Signor Bonetti.

"I think I'd like to meet this guy."

He laughed.

"No. I'm serious. I've never seen anyone stump you. Hell, I've never seen you tired."

He laughed again.

She playfully slapped his biceps. "Come on. I think it would be fun to meet him."

He set his drink on the coffee table. "I know it would be a laugh a minute for you, but it would mess up whatever rapport I've established—or that I'm kidding myself into thinking I've established."

"I might surprise you."

He didn't doubt that for one second. Sometimes she was sunshine in a bottle. Other times she was like Attila the Hun's little sister.

The thought made him laugh again.

"You're going to have to stop laughing at me."

"I'm not laughing at you. I'm laughing with you."

Having fun, he leaned forward and placed a quick kiss on her lips. The automatic reaction stunned them both. It had been nothing but a reflex but the quick touch of his lips to hers felt like coming home. For ten seconds, they looked into each other's eyes, then she leaned forward at the same time he did, and their lips met softly.

But the softness became a frenzy of need. Their mouths opened to allow their tongues to twine, then retreat, so he could nibble her bottom lip. Visions of making love with her returned. The ease and simplicity of their connection filled his chest with longing as their mouths mated. A tsunami of desire overwhelmed him, a yearning so intense that common sense had him breaking away.

She blinked, gazing at him with sleepy green eyes that urged him to kiss her again. But his brain woke. He remembered what a nice person she was. He remembered that her life might be a mess, but that was only temporary. His life was always a mess.

And he'd told her.

He'd confided in her.

He'd put them on the slippery slope of making a genuine connection and now he had to get them off.

"I'm so sorry."

She blinked. Her dreamy expression fled. "What?"

"That was supposed to be a friendly kiss. You know. A peck between friends but there is something powerful in the attraction I feel for you and… Well, I shouldn't have risked even the friendly kiss."

Wyatt understood what he'd been trying to tell her, but even he didn't buy the explanation that had tumbled out. All his life had been about keeping secrets, except from Trace and Cade and now he was telling her things, happy when he saw her with his baby girl and kissing her?

It almost seemed that ignoring their sexual attraction had the unwanted result of real conversations and confidences. Which was weird. He could handle sex. The mindless, easy sex they'd had when they were dating had been fabulous.

But he couldn't handle getting close to her. Not for himself. *For her.* He was a horrible bet as a partner. She deserved better.

"You're saying we're friends?"

"You don't think we are?"

She studied him a second. "I guess spending so much time together we almost have to be."

Relief stuttered through him. "Yes. I think we need to be friends because of Darcy, because I want to help you and because we're in this beautiful place that we should be seeing."

"Seeing?"

"Yes. You know. Sightseeing."

Giving them something to do other than get to know each other, like each other, confide more things that would make them long to indulge their attraction.

She said, "Right," sounding extremely skeptical. He didn't blame her. But keeping them busy sounded like a good plan, and he was sticking to it.

She rose from the sofa. "Goodnight, Wyatt."

CHAPTER SEVEN

SOPHIE WALKED TO her room, shaking her head. "Friendly kiss?" She snorted. *Seriously. Was there even such a thing?*

She didn't think so and Wyatt was only kidding himself if he believed that was what had happened between them. After sliding into pajamas, she got into bed. She could still feel the tingles of excitement that raced through her the second his mouth had met hers. The roar of arousal that had followed still rode her blood.

And he thought they could be friends?

Doubtful.

Oh, *he* might be able to separate friendship and their old relationship, but her hormones were not on board.

She fell into a restless sleep and woke tired the next morning. As if he hadn't kissed her the night before, cheerful Wyatt shooed her out of the nursery and got Darcy ready for the day himself. By the time Sophie got to the breakfast table, Wyatt was eating his eggs and bacon as he fed the baby.

She tried to take the baby spoon from his hand. "Let me do that."

He pulled it away. "We're fine. Ring for Mrs. P. Get your breakfast."

He looked amazing in his white shirt and red tie with the black suit coat hanging on the back of his chair.

Amazing.

Not just good or even attractive. No. He had to look amazing.

Why did the guy she thought the most handsome in the world have to be the one guy she couldn't have?

And why had that guy kissed her?

Because she wasn't buying that friendly kiss explanation.

She grumpily walked back to her chair. "I only get a plate of fruit."

"Maybe if you'd eat a pastry, you'd be happier."

She scowled as she hit the buzzer to ring for the cook. Mrs. P. walked into the dining room all smiles and Sophie realized why her bad mood was so obvious. Everybody around her was happy.

"Are you ready for breakfast, miss?" Mrs. P. asked with so much cheer Sophie almost winced.

Instead, she forced a smiled. "Yes. Thank you."

A few seconds later, Mrs. P. returned with her fruit platter. "I added cinnamon toast."

This time she did wince. Okay. That was confirmation that her mood was obvious. But Wyatt had kissed her—

She sighed. *No. They'd kissed each other.* And that was trouble. Not only had they already been down this road, but also more than kissing was happening on this trip. They were talking. Getting close.

That was when she recognized what was bothering her. He'd told her about getting Darcy. He'd told her about his parents. They were actually discussing Signor Bonetti and his negotiating tactics.

When they'd dated, they'd talked about wine and art, music and dancing, the best places to go in New York City, their favorite plays. They'd never run out of things to talk about. He'd even told her bits and pieces of his work, but he hadn't told her the important things about himself. His fears. His past. His troubles. Now, he was. And easily. As if living together made it perfectly natural for him to confide in her.

She genuinely believed he had no idea all this talking was taking them to a level more important than sex.

And she was going to get hurt.

She had to get herself back on track, get their relationship back on track, start working toward her purposes before she ran out of time.

"How about giving me the contact number for someone in your PR department. I think I need to get that ball rolling."

"I know I suggested that yesterday, but I think it would be smarter for me to call ahead, tell them what you need and have the appropriate person call *you*."

His plate empty, he tossed his napkin to the table, rose, kissed Darcy's forehead and said, "I'm going to phone Trace and Cade this morning. They need an update and maybe they'll have some ideas for how to get Bonetti talking."

With that he left, and Sophie slumped in her chair. Maybe some carbs were in order?

She bit into the cinnamon toast and felt marginally better. But with every bite, she got a little stronger. Or maybe her brain awoke? Like it or not, she had over a week left to deal with Wyatt. And she would do it like a professional.

Not a nitwit, who couldn't see past the fact that he was sexy and good in bed.

Wyatt walked back to the office he'd been using and plopped down on the desk chair. Before he set up the video call with his partners, he read through the financials one more time. It might be ten o'clock in Italy, but it was only four in the morning in Manhattan. He needed to be ready, so he didn't waste the time of his sleep-deprived friends.

Of course, Trace was in Tuscany. So, they were in sync. But even if Cade was on his island in the Florida Keys, he was still six hours behind.

After two hours of reading and making notes, pondering possible stumbling blocks for Bonetti's wanting to sell, he was ready to talk to Trace and Cade. He set his computer for a video call and within seconds their happy faces appeared on the screen. Cade's blond hair was a bit mussed as if he'd just crawled out of bed, but the rolled-up sleeves of Trace's shirt said he was already working. Sundays were one of his vineyard's busiest days.

"Everything okay?"

He sighed and sank back into the chair.

"You're sighing? I thought you'd be happy," Trace said with a laugh. "Lake Como is beautiful."

"It *is* beautiful. We've even taken a boat out."

Cade said, "That's great."

"Yeah, fabulous. The whole reason for my being here is to get a company, not to see the sights."

"Wouldn't hurt to see the sights," Trace pointed out, "if it would improve your sour mood."

"My mood will skyrocket when Signor Bonetti decides he wants to negotiate rather than play golf, introduce me to his family, show me his villa and in general talk about Italian food."

Cade sat up. "He's not negotiating?"

"I have no idea what he's doing. He actually left to visit his grandsons for a day and a half. Told me to see the sights."

"Maybe he doesn't like you grouchy either?"

The comment reminded him of Sophie. When Mrs. P. offered her cinnamon toast, it was clear her mood was apparent to everyone, not just him.

Because he'd kissed her?

Or because he'd brushed it off?

He used the things he'd found in the financials to take the conversation with Trace and Cade in the direction of the purpose for the call. Cade had observations, but Trace's thoughts about Bonetti struck a chord.

"He's clearly hesitant to sell his company. Maybe in the same way Marcia's dad had reservations about selling his vineyard to me."

Knowing the story of Trace's father-in-law, Wyatt said, "You think he's broke? He can't be broke. I read his financials. He's got enough money to support himself and his extended family for the next two generations."

"I'm talking more about pride," Trace said. "Marcia's dad pretended he was happy to be selling out and retiring, but being shoved out of the vineyard he'd nurtured from infancy made him feel small."

"Signor Bonetti does not feel small."

"Oh, you won't see it. He'll pretend for all the world that he's happy. That's how men like him salvage their pride. Watch for little things. Facial tics. A sudden look of sadness that he can't hide."

Wyatt rose from his seat and turned to gaze out the big window behind him. The manicured grounds soothed him, then he saw Sophie walking to the pool, holding a giggling Darcy.

Getting his mind off her bathing suit and back on the conversation with his partners, he said, "You think he doesn't want to sell?"

"I think he *does* want to sell," Trace said, "but maybe he feels odd letting go of his life's work."

"That makes sense."

Cade agreed. "I get that, too. I have a fiancée who won't desert the clientele she built up in our small town in Ohio. We should live in Manhattan…or on the island. Instead, she's caring for the people she loves. Because she's spent five years getting them to trust her and she won't breach that trust."

"See?" Trace said. "We *buy* existing companies so we don't understand the feeling that someone who builds a company from nothing would have when they sell."

"I suppose."

"Maybe be more careful with him?"

"I don't get a chance to be anything with him. He calls the shots."

Cade laughed. "I'd pay to see that."

"Very funny."

"You do have a tendency to be bossy," Trace reminded him.

He looked at Sophie, watched her slide Darcy through the water. He thought of how he'd kept their relationship in a neat little box three years ago so he could get what he wanted. "Maybe a little."

"And contrary to your beliefs, you're not always right."

Holding Darcy by the tummy, swishing her along the blue water, Sophie turned in a circle, showing him all sides of her perfect body in a little yellow swimsuit.

When he didn't laugh at Cade's snarky observation, Cade said, "What are you looking at?"

He pulled himself away from the window, sat at the desk and faced Cade and Trace again. "The nanny has the baby in the pool. I was just watching to make sure she was being safe with her."

"You hired a nanny?"

"You told me I had to."

"Well, that's good."

"Yeah, if she's careful with Darcy."

Trace shook his head. "Careful is sometimes your middle name, Wyatt, and though it's prudent to be safe, sometimes you've gotta take a risk. Get Bonetti talking about how he started the business," he said as he reached for the button to disconnect the call. "Then get back to us. I'll bet you'll have better news."

With that he ended the call.

Cade said, "I agree," then he disconnected too.

Wyatt pulled in a breath and swiveled his chair toward the window again. It was a hot day. Bonetti probably expected him to shuffle over and beg for his attention.

Well, Trace wanted him to take some risks? Maybe he would.

He called Bonetti, told him he wouldn't be over that day and headed upstairs to change into swimming trunks.

When he reached the pool, Sophie was twisting the baby, almost spinning her.

Terrified, he raced down the ladder. "What are you doing?"

"It's called a vertical spin. I saw it online. It's supposed to show her that the water doesn't have to control her. She can move in the water."

He took the baby from Sophie only to discover that Darcy was calm and happy. She babbled a few lines that sounded like an attempt to explain something to him.

Wyatt shook his head. "You liked being spun?"

Darcy grinned.

He glanced at Sophie. "Okay, maybe you have a point."

"There's tons of stuff on the internet about teaching babies to swim. Even if you aren't comfortable with it now, when she's only a few months old, at the very least getting her accustomed to the water, to moving in the water, will help her when you do think she's old enough."

"How young are the kids learning to swim in the videos you saw?"

"Six months. Eight months."

"Then she's old enough."

Sophie shrugged. "Yes. But…" She shrugged again. "Why rush things? Getting her accustomed to the water, to playing in the water, to seeing the water as fun might be as far as you need to go right now."

He totally relaxed then realized he'd tensed because he didn't want to push Darcy to do anything. His parents had pushed him his entire childhood—

He wouldn't let his mind take that unhappy trip. Not on such a beautiful day. Not when he'd finally called the shots with Signor Bonetti.

He looked around, let the greenery and blue sky calm him. "It's a perfect day."

"It is." She walked through the water to him. "Let me take her."

She reached out to take Darcy and their arms brushed. Electricity sprinted through him. He pretended he didn't feel it, though he let her take the baby.

He expected her to say something about him giving up the little girl so easily.

She didn't.

He relaxed some more. The baby giggled in Sophie's arms as she glided her through the water again, even doing the spin thing that had scared him. The sun beat down on him. The peace of the place filled him.

"I think I'll swim."

Sophie laughed. "You don't have to ask. Just swim."

He pushed off on his toes and dove across the three-foot water into the deeper area where he swam laps until he relaxed into a backstroke with a satisfied "Ahh."

"This place is more than pretty. Look around. There's so much to do. Places to walk and gather your thoughts. Tennis courts with ball returns so you can play alone. A basketball court. You could shoot hoops."

He didn't know why but hearing her say, "Shoot hoops," sounded funny.

"Do *you* shoot hoops?"

"Not really, but that's all the guys in my old neighborhood did."

He drifted closer to her and the baby.

"I'd watch them out the window."

He could see her, alone while her dad worked, not allowed outside where there was trouble. His heart did a little shimmy of sorrow for her, so he decided to steer clear of that part of the experience and took the conversation in the opposite direction.

"Didn't you learn anything from watching them?"

She laughed.

He shifted from the backstroke to treading water and reached for Darcy. "Give her to me."

She handed the baby over. Only their hands touched, but his skin prickled at her nearness. Their gazes caught. Their old connection arched between them, initiated, he was sure, by their easy conversation and the very natural way they were treating each other. Just like when they were lovers.

Baby securely in his arms, he eased into the deeper water again. He watched Sophie as she made a move to follow them, but hesitated.

He put his attention on Darcy as he casually

said, "You know, if we'd let go the next few days, and just sleep together, we'd probably both be a lot happier."

He expected a horrified gasp. Instead, she ran her hand through the water.

Interesting.

Reading into her reaction, he said, "You've thought about it."

She took a breath.

"Wow. You've thought about it a lot."

Her gaze leapt to his. "So I've thought about it? But I thought about it…more as memories not planning for the future."

He laughed. "Memories *are* planning for the future."

Her face scrunched. "How do you get that?"

"You think about what was because you're really thinking about what could be."

He watched her eyes change as she understood his meaning. Then she trudged over to the pool's ladder. "Well, that just makes it official. I shouldn't have come."

That was the last thing he'd expected her to say. She was the perfect nanny. He'd been the perfect employer. Only their attraction messed things up. And he had a solution for that.

"Come on. Come back in the pool. I think we need to talk about this."

She grabbed a towel. "You act like these two

weeks are time stolen. Like we can do anything we want and just go home and pretend everything's normal. But I'm going home to trouble. I don't need to be pining for you on top of it."

Two things hit him simultaneously. First, he'd thought suggesting that they sleep together was sort of funny, a way to get it all out in the open, and yeah maybe nudge them in the direction of doing it.

She clearly had not.

Second, she *was* going home to trouble.

He slogged through the water to the ladder. "You're right."

She stopped drying herself with the big fluffy towel. "I'm right? Mr. I-know-what's-best-for-everybody is admitting he's wrong?"

"I didn't say I was wrong. I said you were right."

She only frowned at him.

"I still think we should sleep together. But I also see you've got some things to do before you can go home. Since I decided to ditch Bonetti today, we can go inside and call my PR department."

"It's Sunday."

"They're go-getters. Lots of them come in for a few hours, even on weekends. We'll set up a Zoom call to talk about the statement you'll need and also have them coach you on attitude and appearance. They'll show you how things you might do naturally can be perceived and then demonstrate how you should behave so you don't stand out in the crowd. You don't want to appear arrogant when you're doing something simple like getting your morning coffee."

The relief on her face showed just how worried she was about going home. He should have seen it or thought of it sooner, but he hadn't. While she'd been taking excellent care of Darcy, he'd sort of left her hanging out to dry.

Because he'd been afraid of their attraction.

But he wasn't anymore. And he would show her she didn't have to be either.

CHAPTER EIGHT

THE CALL WAS incredibly helpful. If Sophie had ever doubted the importance of a PR department, she had been converted to the other side. After hearing her part in the story of her mom's arrest, how she was innocent, merely house-sitting a condo, Wyatt's team made suggestions on how often to appear in public and even where to go. Coffee shops were good. Expensive restaurants were not. And no shopping trips. She didn't even want to give the appearance that she was spending money her mother had stolen.

She could have told them they need not worry about that. She had no money. She would not be shopping. But she kept her mouth shut and listened more than she spoke because that was how smart people learned.

After twenty more minutes of teaching her how to say, "No comment," without looking rude or condescending, the job of crafting her statement was assigned to a youngish-looking guy who promised he would get back to her on Monday.

She thought the conversation was over, but Wyatt went into detail about what he expected the statement to accomplish and while her eyebrows rose at his high expectations, his staff nodded and told him he'd get everything he wanted.

Of course, he would.

Not only was he the boss but his life seemed to be geared toward success. Sometimes it was almost fun watching fate turn into favor for him.

She remembered how much she'd loved that when they were dating, then memories poured into her brain like gentle rain, filling her chest with longing. She'd liked them together. They weren't exactly yin and yang, but they complemented each other. He was forceful. She was more subtle. She could pull him out of a bad mood. He could get her to come out of her shell.

He'd never thought of her as anything less than his equal. Despite her humble beginnings, they had been partners.

She'd missed that and the reminder only served to make her long for their connection.

He was feeling it too. He'd as much as said it in the pool, but his recollections seemed to be more sexual.

While hers were wistful. He was the guy of her dreams. Strong. Determined. Able to get things done. And romantic. He could be such a romantic when wooing her.

She almost sighed.

"So, everybody's got a job to do."

The people at the big conference table in his office nodded and said words of agreement.

"Okay, then. Get it done."

The simple way he commanded his staff sent that weird tingle through her and she understood what he'd been saying in the pool about their sexual tension, except she would add an "or" to his proposition. Either they had to indulge the sexual needs that wove through their conversations and daily dealings, *or* they had to stop spending so much time together.

The second choice seemed like the wiser one.

She rose from the seat across from him in the office of the villa. "You know what? I think I'm going to take the rest of the day off."

He blinked. "What?"

"You're here. You've got things under control. I just want to sightsee."

"I could—"

"You could stay with the baby."

He tossed his pen to the desk. From the expression in his eyes, she knew he was figuring things out, reasoning why she might want time on her own. "Our conversation in the pool isn't making you run away, is it?"

"Nope. Not running. Just want to see the sights."

He shook his head as if confused. "Alone?"

"There's nothing wrong with being alone." She took a breath. "Why don't you think of it as me needing a little time off after working five days with barely a break."

That struck the chord. "Oh. Geez. I'm sorry. You're working twenty-four-seven and right now I'm here to care for Darcy. You could get a break." He waved his hand. "Go. Enjoy."

"I'll be home in time to put her to bed."

"No. Don't worry about that. We're fine. Go. Have a good time. You can take one of the cars in the garage or if you don't want to drive on roads that you're unfamiliar with, Marco, the gardener is also the driver. I'm sure he'll be happy to take you to Bellagio."

"Thanks." She left to go to the kitchen to ask Mrs. P. how to arrange for a ride into town and Mrs. P. said she would handle telling Marco.

After almost an hour to shower, fix her hair and put on a sundress, she was in a car being driven to town. That part felt weird. But otherwise, happiness buzzed through her. She was in Italy. About to tour the most beautiful small town she had ever seen. Yes, in a little over a week she'd be going home to a disaster, but right now, she was in Italy. She intended to enjoy it.

She spent the first hour ducking down cobblestone alleys with quaint shops, refusing to let her fun be stolen by thoughts of her mother and all the prep work she'd have to do with Wyatt's staff to get herself ready to deal with her mother's scandal.

But it wasn't easy. Almost a week had gone by. In another week, she'd be returning to her mother's mess made worse by the fact that she loved being Darcy's nanny and would miss her... and Wyatt.

Their relationship had ended in her heartbreak, but he had so many redeeming qualities. He was helping her. He loved Darcy. He trusted her with Darcy. He made her laugh. They could talk about things, even more than when they were together. He'd actually told her about his parents and Darcy's mother. Things he never would have done three years ago. And when they parted company, she would miss him.

The realization didn't surprise her, but as she walked through gaggles of tourists and past hand-holding lovers, she suddenly missed him *now*. They were like sunshine and blue skies. They fit. It was hell to be together but hold back saying things, *feeling* things. She saw him every morning, saw him when he returned from work, saw him when they put Darcy to bed together and she thought of him when she settled into her lonely bed—

The strangest thought hit her. No matter what happened between them, she would miss him. She wouldn't miss him any less if she spent the next week avoiding him. Or any more if they slept together.

Whatever happened, she would miss him.

Wanting to put her mind anywhere else than on Wyatt and the crystal-clear thoughts that began to haunt her, she considered buying a souvenir but decided to spend her money at the pastry shop she and Wyatt had visited. Right before she called Marco to return to collect her, she would indulge in one of those delicious desserts. That wouldn't be too much to put on her credit card, but it would make the late afternoon feel special.

Her plan made, she continued toward the town square. Tree-lined streets and statues took her attention to the point that she forgot to look where she was and simply wandered. Eventually, she found the Basilica of St. Giacomo and gaped for a minute at the gorgeous stone structure before she stepped inside.

Shimmering silence greeted her, along with a golden altar surrounded by a stone wall that formed a half circle. Ancient, but well-kept wooden furniture caught the colors that danced in through stained-glass windows. Stone walls and golden frames displayed paintings of angels and saints.

The perfection of it nearly overwhelmed her.

She glanced around. She'd never seen anything like it. She'd lived a small life until her mom bought her a condo and she and Wyatt started their affair. He'd opened up so much of the world to her and now he was doing it again. Just by giving her the opportunity to be at Lake Como for two weeks, he was showing her more of the world.

Damned if it didn't give her the feeling that she was thinking too small, letting her troubles control her.

She couldn't change the fact that her mom was in jail. She would have to answer questions. But she didn't have to cower or be afraid. She'd done nothing wrong.

And, damn it, she wasn't letting her life stop because her biological mom was a thief.

She walked out of the basilica laughing. She wasn't sure if it was letting a little time pass or if being with Wyatt had given her perspective, but she suddenly understood. She'd spent her entire life without her mother. She didn't have to either persecute her *or* help her. What she needed to do was take care of herself, take care of her own business to get her life back on track again.

Strolling to the bakery, she waited for more clarity about school, about money, about where she should live but none came. Still, she had a week before she had to make any decisions.

She took a seat at one of the outdoor tables, and a waiter hastened over to help her. She didn't speak Italian, so he shifted to broken English, which was charming but also reminded her that when they needed to smart people adjusted.

This time she chose a buttery cookie, buying six of them so she'd have some to take back to the villa. She ordered coffee, despite the late hour, and settled in to enjoy the scenery while she waited for her treat.

"Of all the—"

She glanced up to see Wyatt standing by her two-person table. He took a seat on the wrought iron chair across from hers. "I wasn't following you. I swear."

"You're supposed to be home."

He laughed. "I was. But after volunteering to watch the baby, Mrs. P. shooed me out. Said I'd have eighteen years with Darcy but how many times would I get to Lake Como."

"You told her you're rich, right?"

"Didn't seem to impress her."

She chuckled, but her heart swelled with that feeling she'd had as she wandered around Bellagio. It didn't matter if she and Wyatt spent no more time together, she would miss him when they returned home.

And even if it was wrong, she wanted to be with him—enjoy this chance she never thought she'd get.

"I actually ordered six cookies."

"Did you now?"

"I'd intended to take five of them back to the house as treats throughout the rest of the week."

"Then I won't take one."

"No, you probably should." She smiled across the table at him. "Besides, I like to share."

"I do remember that about you. You're one of the most generous people I know."

"You have your moments too."

He laughed.

And the world suddenly seemed to right itself.

"If you're really here to sightsee, I just spent an hour in Basilica of St. Giacomo. I wouldn't mind going back for a second look, if you'd like to see it."

"Really? You'd join me?"

"Well, let's see how many cookies you eat first."

He laughed again and the world righted itself a little more.

"I actually had some moments of clarity there."

"Oh?"

The waiter came, set the cookies on the table between them and gave Sophie her coffee.

"Another coffee for me, please," Wyatt said

before he lifted a cookie. "What were your profound revelations?"

"Really just one big revelation."

"And?"

"I realized I hadn't done anything wrong, so I didn't need to cower or be afraid."

He nodded. "Time away was a good thing for you after all."

She winced. "That and listening to your PR staff. I'm not sure I'd be so comfortable standing tall without their talking points and guidance about keeping a low profile without staying out of sight."

"They are good."

"You trained them well."

"No. I was talking about the cookies. Eat one so I can eat another."

She rolled her eyes but took a cookie.

"Oh, wow."

He pulled in a breath as he looked around. "I'd say we have to come here again some time, but I guess we only have another a week in Italy. I'll probably spend most of it with Bonetti."

Just like that her bubble burst.

Or maybe she had another moment of clarity. They had a few days together and she wanted them. She wanted time with him and Darcy, fun in the swimming pool, and romantic nights.

And she was going after it.

CHAPTER NINE

AFTER A TRIP to the basilica, where Sophie all but gave Wyatt a guided tour, they knew it was time to head home. Walking through town to the parking lot where he'd left the car, he gave her his phone so she could call Mrs. P. who agreed to tell Marco she didn't need a ride home.

He held the door for her and she climbed into the little red convertible sports car. When he sat behind the steering wheel, she smiled over at him, warming his heart.

"You're always taking me places or showing me new things."

He maneuvered the car through the streets until he got them to the road that would return them to the villa. She'd been happy all evening, which made him happy, and caused the cascade of wonderful memories he had every time he was around her.

"I have access to more things," he said.

"And you're not afraid to try new stuff."

He peered over. "You're not afraid either."

She took a breath. "That's the new plan."

They spent the balance of the drive discussing fear and life and how smart people go after what they want. He was working to reinforce her decision to take charge of her life when they returned to Manhattan. But he got the impression the conversation meant something totally different to her.

He let her out at the front door, then drove the convertible into the garage. Silence greeted him when he walked into the house and up the short hall to the foyer.

About to start up the steps to his bedroom, he stopped dead when she called to him from the drawing room off to the left.

"I poured you a bourbon."

He turned from the stairs. "You did?"

"And a glass of wine for myself."

Their ritual.

When they were dating and they'd returned from an event, he'd check his phone before he turned it off, while she poured him a bourbon and herself a glass of wine. Then they'd sit in the living room and sip their drinks. To decompress she'd say.

But he always managed to seduce her, lure her back to the bedroom, and their glasses would sit forgotten on his coffee table.

He licked his suddenly dry lips.

She smiled and displayed the short glass with a splash of amber liquid on ice.

Too intrigued to walk away, he entered the living room and took the drink she offered him.

He sat on the sofa. She sat beside him.

"You liked the basilica?"

He let his gaze drift to hers. "I like everything about Lake Como." And he liked her. Always had.

He'd broken up with her to save her but tonight she didn't look like a woman who needed saving.

She took a sip of wine. "You really should buy a second home here."

"I'll have Trace run some numbers."

She laughed and turned to face him, her elbow on the back of the sofa. "For what? You have plenty of money."

"Yes." He glanced down at his bourbon. "But a smart person doesn't jump into things."

She smiled. "Why not?"

"Risk."

"You can afford to lose a few million dollars."

His skin began to tingle from her nearness. "Not all risk is about money."

"What do you think you'll lose by buying a house? If you change your mind, you can always sell it. Not everything is meant to be permanent."

He glanced over at her. "No. I guess not."

"And sometimes," she said, her gaze firmly holding his. "Things come into our lives for periods of time, or for reasons, or to help us through something. The trick is to enjoy them, then be able to let them go."

He studied her face, full lips, pert nose, serious eyes.

He was just about certain he knew what she was telling him and while part of him wanted to slide his fingers into the thick hair at the back of her head to hold her still so he could kiss her senseless, the other part held back.

She quietly said, "You're helping me a lot."

"It's what good people do."

She set her glass on the coffee table and faced him fully. "Exactly. You had the ability to help me, and you did. Now we're in this beautiful part of the world where we're having fun with your daughter and remembering all the good things we did together."

He said nothing, only watched her.

"You said it yourself this afternoon."

"I did."

She rose from the sofa. He sat back, watching as she unbuttoned the two closures at the top of her dress, then reached down to pull it over her head, revealing a pink bra and panties.

His breath stuttered.

She straddled him. Her wavy yellow hair drifted around her. "You said you wanted to get rid of the tension between us."

"We were doing okay in Bellagio tonight."

She laughed. "You've never been able to resist me, and I've barely been able to resist you... and we have a few days. No promises. No regrets. Some of the best things in life are temporary."

She leaned in and kissed him, and he let himself tumble over the edge. He speared the fingers of his right hand into her hair while his left hand undid the hooks of her bra, tossed it away and flattened against her naked back to press her to him.

That's when he realized he was fully clothed, and she was virtually naked. Every atom in his body had expanded with need and he sat there in a layer of clothes. She placed her hands on his cheeks to kiss him fully and he took advantage, unbuttoning his shirt and undoing his belt. Then he tipped her to lie on the sofa, giving himself space to remove his shirt and pants.

Finally happy, he leaned down and grazed his hands along the curve of her waist, up to her breasts and back down again. He'd never been so desperate or so hungry and when his fingers met the silk of her panties, they didn't pause. He yanked the little pink triangles down as he leaned in to run his lips over her torso.

Somehow, she flipped their positions, easing him down so she could reach him. They touched and tasted each other, both a little desperate with need and reverent with the sense of disbelief. He never thought he'd touch her again. Not even when he'd made the suggestion in the pool. But here they were.

When he finally joined them, he took a minute to savor. What he felt for her went beyond simple need. He liked her. His emotions went further than what he felt for his friends, beyond what he'd ever felt for another woman, but he wouldn't call it love because love was a tarnished word to him.

So, he worshipped her with himself. He took them to a place where want and need collided and then exploded in a shower of perfection.

Then they went to his room and did it again. They didn't talk. They lingered, their actions speaking much louder than words ever could.

Sophie woke the next morning to the sense of coming home. Not a feeling of déjà vu at being in Wyatt's bed content and happy, but a perception that she had come back to where she belonged. She knew this wasn't forever. But what was? Her mother's love had barely lasted through her toddler years. Her dad had moved on with his new family. Her house sitting job had been three years then done.

Plus, she and Wyatt always seemed to have a shelf life. This time it was two weeks and one of those weeks was already gone.

She could make more of this than it meant to him. Or she could enjoy what they had. Take memories back to Manhattan with her. Then use them to help her get through the rough weeks when she got home and the even rougher year it would take to finish school while she struggled to find loans and grants and waited tables to make her rent.

That would be the smart move. And if there was one thing she was learning on this trip to Italy it was that she was smart. She didn't have to be timid. She didn't have to think herself less than because her mother had abandoned her. She was fine...just the way she was.

Realizing Wyatt was spooned around her, she smiled.

He nuzzled her neck. "Good morning."

She turned in his arms. "Good morning."

"I didn't hear the baby last night."

She winced. "I got up with her twice. Once

there was a disaster in her diaper. Once she wanted to eat."

He laughed. "So maybe it was lucky I didn't hear her."

She nipped a kiss on his lips. "Or preplanned." She slid out of bed. "We have a choice. Quickly shower and hope she doesn't wake up. Or go wake her and start the day."

He rolled out of bed. Gloriously naked, he stepped into a pair of sweats. "I'll get her. You shower."

Surprised, she frowned. "Really?" He never missed a chance at shower sex.

"Of course, it *is* only six," he said casually. "If we hurried, we could probably shower and be out before she wakes."

"She was up at five. She's probably got another good hour of sleep in her."

He headed for the bathroom. "Let's not waste a minute."

She walked into the glass and shiny white tile shower. He followed her in and turned her around for a blistering kiss. The night before, he'd let her take the lead. This morning he was totally in command. Hot kisses morphed into a steamy trail of bites down her neck, as his hands roamed every inch of her.

When she tried to touch him, he held her hands behind her back, as if telling her he wanted his fun now. She let him have his way until they were both breathless with need then he pressed her against the shower wall and took her.

After a second session, she shared the shower spray with him, quickly washed her hair and got out, so she could tend to the baby.

She grabbed a fluffy towel to dry herself and the sounds of Darcy crying suddenly erupted from the baby monitor. "I'll get her."

She turned and reached for...nothing.

"I forgot! I don't have clothes!"

He stepped into the sweats again. "That's okay. You go to your room to dress. I'll get the baby."

Though it only took her ten minutes to comb out her hair and slip into a T-shirt and shorts, the nursery was empty by the time she arrived.

She raced downstairs to find happy Darcy in the highchair and Wyatt sitting at the head of the table, a T-shirt added to his sweatpants.

"That was fast."

She flipped her wet hair over her shoulder. "That's the good thing about long hair. I can let it air dry."

Mrs. P. walked in. "Good morning, Sophie. The usual?"

Wyatt intervened. "I think she should have pancakes this morning."

She gasped. "I haven't had pancakes in years."

Casually spooning some rice cereal into Darcy's open mouth, Wyatt said, "Three years, I'll bet."

She laughed, remembering how he could get her to eat pancakes every Sunday morning when she would have chosen fruit. "That might be a good thing."

"Not when you use a lot of energy." He fed Darcy another bite. "And sightseeing last night had us walking everywhere."

She smiled at Mrs. P. "Pancakes it is."

As the cook left, Wyatt said, "So what's on your agenda for today?"

"I was going to ask you the same thing."

"I'll probably see Bonetti. Listen to stories about his life. Trace said to try to get him talking about starting his business but any time I mention his business he ignores me."

She laughed. "Why don't you turn the tables and start talking about your life? Tell him stories about Darcy, your friends, Cade's island, Trace's vineyard."

His coffee cup stopped midway to his mouth. "That's not such a bad idea."

"You once told me that mimicking is a negotiating tool."

"It is."

"So use it. Talk about what he talks about."

He set his coffee cup on the saucer. "I don't normally talk about myself."

"Maybe that's what he's waiting for?"

"Trace thinks he's having trouble selling his company. His baby."

She shrugged. "Maybe. Or maybe he's been trying to draw you out so he can see who he's selling his company to."

He grimaced. "I should rephrase what I said before. I don't *like* talking about myself."

"Yeah, no kidding." She took a quick breath. "Keep the conversation on your friendships with your partners. After all, it's three of you buying the company. Talk about Cade. Talk about Trace. Talk about your friendship. Your bond."

Even as she said that the doorbell chimed. A minute later, Mrs. P. walked into the dining room with a short bald man.

Wyatt rose. "Mr. Bonetti."

Sophie's eyebrows shot up, but Bonetti grinned. "Good morning."

He motioned to Sophie who wasn't quite sure if she should rise and stay seated or bow. He looked like an aging statesman who deserved the respect.

"This is Sophie Sanders, Darcy's nanny." He pointed to the baby in the highchair. "And this is Darcy." He paused a second as Bonetti took the seat beside Sophie. "Would you like some coffee?"

"Yes. Thank you."

Wyatt nodded to Mrs. P., indicating he would get the coffee and she left the room.

"What brings you here?"

"I love this villa. I wanted to be sure you were comfortable."

Or he was checking up on them.

Wyatt poured the coffee and served it to Bonetti. "Sophie's been telling me I should buy it."

Bonetti laughed.

"I think his partners would really like it," Sophie interjected before Wyatt could say anything else. "Trace actually owns a vineyard in Tuscany. Cade's more of an all-American. He owns an island with a beach house."

Bonetti's thick, black eyebrows rose. "Oh?"

"Both are engaged. Trace's fiancée is general manager of his vineyard. Cade's fiancée owns a home nursing agency."

Bonetti nodded.

"They are great guys. Smart but normal. You know, they like boating and watching sports, as much as they like running big companies."

Wyatt stared at Sophie. Though Cade and Trace believed Bonetti was being nostalgic about selling the company he'd built, the old man seemed to be extremely interested in what Sophie was saying. As if she'd been correct, Bonetti wanted to know some personal details about the people seeking to buy his life's work.

He fed Darcy another spoonful of cereal, remembering again how smart Sophie was as she continued to tell Bonetti things about Trace and Cade, things she remembered from when she'd met them. Things he'd told her in passing.

The interesting thing about Sophie was that she was so accustomed to being observant and putting two and two together that she never saw how intelligent she was. Or, maybe more important, she didn't realize how rare it was that someone could use their intelligence so practically.

Bonetti stayed an hour, letting Wyatt take Darcy upstairs for her morning nap, while he continued to chitchat with Sophie.

When he returned downstairs, Bonetti was gone and Sophie was grinning. "He said he'll see you at his house when you're ready to come over."

He returned to his seat at the breakfast table. "Thanks."

Sophie's grin grew. "He seemed more than interested in your partners."

"And you were doing a great job talking about them, so I let you run with the ball."

"It was fun."

"And you were aces at it." He wanted to tell her he now owed her, but he knew she'd brush that off. "I wish you'd let me help you." The words were out of his mouth before he realized he'd even formed them. But now that they were out, he stood by them.

"You are helping me."

"The only thing you'll seem to let me do is give you access to my PR department."

"Hey, bud, don't forget you're paying me a salary for being Darcy's nanny. And I expect a pretty penny. Enough for first month's rent and security deposit for a halfway decent apartment."

He hadn't forgotten. He just wasn't sure how much he could pay her before she'd have a hissy fit and refuse his generosity.

"If you'd let me, I could put in a good word for you with one of my business acquaintances to get you a job as an assistant so you could finish university."

"Oh, I plan to finish."

He remembered her saying that the trip had given her clarity. It looked like school had factored into that.

She took a sip of coffee, then said, "I worked all that out yesterday."

"While you were sightseeing?"

"Yes. With a clear head, I recognized I could

get grants and loans like everybody else. I'll be filling out applications while Darcy naps today. I didn't come this far to quit."

His heart stumbled with relief. "I could actually pay you enough that it would cover your rent for a year."

She set her fork down and sighed. "Wyatt. I have to do this myself."

"Why?"

"Because you're not my reality."

His face scrunched. "Did you just say I'm not real?"

She snorted. "No. I'm saying that when we return to Manhattan, we will not be in the same world. You'll be working in Manhattan. I can't afford to live there, so God knows where I'll end up. But we'll probably never see each other again once we return to the States."

Though that thought had flirted with entering his brain, he'd never allowed it to fully form. Oh, he knew it was true, but he didn't want to think about it.

Or ponder how easy it seemed to be for her to accept it.

"Truth be told, this whole trip isn't my reality. I was lucky that you came up to my apartment and caught me when I was so gobsmacked I could barely think. I'd have been drowning in trouble right now if I'd stayed in New York. So though other people might consider this side trip delaying the inevitable, to me it was lucky you stepped in and offered me this job. A chance to get away to think and make some money."

At least she called it lucky that he'd offered her a job.

He stared at his empty coffee cup. "Darcy and I needed you too."

She grinned. "See? Lucky." Her smile dimmed a bit. "But when we get home, reality returns. I have to be prepared for that. Ready to stand on my own two feet."

There were so many ways he could help her, so many things he could do. It made his chest ache that she wouldn't let him do any of those, even as it made him extremely proud of her.

She'd come to terms with this and after a few days of looking for loans and grants and working with his PR team, she would be ready to go home.

He suddenly understood that was what her seduction the night before was all about.

She'd decided to enjoy what was left of their trip because when she got home, reality would hit. And hit hard.

As someone who liked her and understood her problems, he had to support her. He couldn't argue with her. He couldn't suggest alternatives to her plan.

He would go home to his penthouse that was like a palace, with a baby who loved him, two friends who supported him…

While she went home to trouble.

Only a selfish idiot would mess with what was undoubtedly a fragile peace she'd made with herself and her future.

CHAPTER TEN

Around noon, Wyatt left for Bonetti's. Sophie took Darcy for a stroll around the grounds, promising her a swim later that afternoon. The baby babbled and giggled and in general tired herself out. When Sophie took her upstairs to the nursery and fed her a bottle, the little girl immediately fell into a deep sleep.

Sophie leaned back in the rocking chair, staring at Darcy's beautiful face. Feelings she'd been avoiding with Wyatt's baby girl crept up on her. The warmth of love filled her chest, along with the desire for Darcy to have every good thing in life, and a protectiveness that shocked her.

Which made her wonder about her own mother. Darcy wasn't even her child, yet Sophie would face the forces of hell if anyone tried to hurt her. She couldn't imagine Darcy's mother simply deciding one day that she'd rather have a career than raise her child.

Yet, that's what she'd done.

That's what Sophie's mother had also done.

Maybe that was the connection she felt with Darcy now? Not maternal instinct but normal protectiveness. Sophie understood abandonment. She knew the deep hurt. The questions that bubbled up when she'd seen her friends shopping with their moms or dancing around their kitchens. She hadn't had that closeness and never would. She knew the emptiness of that loss and internally railed against Darcy someday facing that.

Of course, Wyatt might dance in the kitchen with his little girl. She also could see him taking Darcy shopping and sitting in a chair outside a waiting room holding her jacket.

Even without a mother, Darcy would have what Sophie never had. A place. While Sophie's dad struggled just to put food on the table, working long hours and sometimes two jobs, Wyatt called the shots in his life.

Something that felt a lot like self-pity tried to rise, but she reminded herself it was fate, luck of the draw who her parents were. She'd accepted that at fourteen. She'd used the knowledge to make herself stronger.

Plus, she loved her dad. Always had. Always would. He'd simply moved on, as a normal guy should. With a wife and two kids and a new mortgage there wasn't time or room for her in his life.

As Darcy slept on her arm, she allowed herself to realize just how strong a woman had to be to look around for the silver lining in her chaos—to choose to recognize that she had more than lots of people had and needed to take what she'd been given and make the best life possible.

She reveled in that strength, thanked God she had that strength and knew right then and there that no matter what happened, she would survive.

The baby snuggled against her, and her heart warmed as her chest filled with love. She might not get things the way other women got them, but she had time with two people she loved. Wyatt and Darcy.

She would only be kidding herself if she thought she didn't love them. This was her space of time to enjoy that. Not just Wyatt, but the baby too.

A whisp of common sense tried to remind her this was a slippery slope. She remembered how hard it had been to get over losing Wyatt—losing the baby would make it impossibly hard, but she shoved those thoughts away.

She was making memories. That was all.

She would need them for the difficult few years she had ahead of her.

* * *

Wyatt sat on a sofa in Signor Bonetti's huge office. Dark wood paneling covered the walls, a brown leather sofa and chair served as a conference area and a huge mahogany desk sat along the back window, behind a dark red oriental rug.

He'd been in a hundred offices like this. The workplaces of men on the verge or retiring, letting go of their life's work, accepting their accomplishments—big or small—as their legacy because they were done.

Some wanted to kick back and enjoy their upcoming free time. Some knew their best years were behind them. Others wanted their company to go on, strong and healthy. Not teetering because of mediocre leadership.

When Bonetti walked over to him from behind the desk and handed him the new five-year plan created by his employees, Wyatt knew that Sophie's chat that morning about Trace and Cade, and the friendship Wyatt shared with them, had resolved some of Bonetti's concerns about whether Three Musketeers Holdings could keep his company solvent.

But he realized two more things. First, Signor Bonetti wanted his company to outlive him. Second, Bonetti had been stalling this past week while his employees finished the financial forecast that outlined what Bonetti wanted his company to accomplish in the next five years.

"This is ambitious."

Bonetti's eyes shined. "You cannot accomplish that?"

"Oh, my partners and I can pretty much do anything we set our minds to."

"Then, we are ready to discuss terms?"

"Yes and no." Wyatt glanced down at the small booklet in front of him. "First, we're going to have to talk money. There's no way we're giving your family twenty-five percent of the profits of a company we'll be running without them." He looked up at Bonetti. "If that's a deal breaker, I can go home now."

"I need to take care of my children."

"You're asking for billions of dollars for this business. Invest it wisely, and generations of Bonettis will live happily-ever-after."

Bonetti laughed. "Should be true. But you don't know my kids."

Wyatt rose. "And I don't intend to support them." He plucked his suit coat off the back of his chair and slid into it, then picked up his copy of the five-year plan. "I don't want to make promises or draw lines until I've read this. But let me give you a piece of advice. Teach your kids how to invest…or put the money in trust for them."

He said the last to give Bonetti some guidance that might ease his mind enough to accept the offer Wyatt was pretty sure he'd be making. But he didn't want to say anything definitive, not even to himself, until he read the five-year plan.

"I'll see you tomorrow."

Bonetti rose. "Okay. Tomorrow."

He returned to the villa and found Sophie and Darcy in the pool. He walked outside, loosening his tie. "If you don't mind, I'm going to spend the afternoon reading this." He displayed the five-year plan.

She swirled Darcy through the water, earning a giggle. "No. We don't mind. Go. Do whatever."

He returned the house and walked straight to the office. After hanging his jacket on the back of a chair and draping his tie over that, he took a seat behind the desk and began reading.

Though the plan was detailed, it only took about two hours to read it and realize that Bonetti wanted Three Musketeers Holdings to keep the company pretty much the way it was. Which was ridiculous. The point of buying a big company like Bonetti's was to improve on it.

He skimmed the whole plan again and when he let go of his own agenda and simply looked for Bonetti's, he realized the old man didn't merely want to assure his kids and their kids and their kids would forever be rich. He also wanted his current employees to have job security.

It was a great idea. Actually, it showed Bonetti was a kind man.

But business was business. He probably would keep most of Bonetti's employees. But he couldn't promise anyone forever.

No one could.

The thought gave him a funny feeling in his gut. He knew that was true. So why did it feel odd, out of place?

A sound had his head jerking up and he looked at the door to see Sophie holding Darcy. "She's going down for her second nap."

He nodded, but also allowed his gaze to take a quick tour of Sophie's long legs.

If she noticed, she didn't show it as she casually said, "Did you have lunch?"

"No. I basically bugged out of Bonetti's to get home to read the five-year plan he wants us to follow."

"Can a guy really tell you how he wants his company run after you buy it?"

"He can tell us anything. The real bottom line to an agreement is enforcement."

"Oh."

"Don't think I'd buy his company and then disregard an agreement to follow his five-year plan. There's integrity involved too."

She smiled.

For some reason, a wave of pride poured

through him. She always seemed to see the best in him, or maybe bring out the best in him. Which was one of the reasons he enjoyed having her around. He'd worked for decades not to turn into his dad. She reminded him he hadn't.

"Anyway, I'm taking the baby to the nursery." As if on cue, Darcy rubbed her eyes sleepily. "Wanna kiss her good-night?"

He rose, walked over and kissed Darcy's forehead. "I'll see you later."

She snuggled into Sophie's chest.

Memories of their night before and morning in the shower rippled through him. He wanted more. Not just sex. But time. He wanted to laugh and talk and let his brain forget about the Bonetti family and their big dreams of being rich forever without doing anything.

"You and I should go out to dinner tonight."

She caught his gaze. "We could."

"Yeah. We could. When she gets up, I'll spend a few hours with her. Then we can leave her with Mrs. P. and head into town."

Just the thought made him feel ridiculous things. Happy. Content. Normal.

Happy and content he understood. Normal perplexed him. How could he feel normal when he had no idea what normal was?

He didn't have time or mental energy to debate it in his brain. He simply let it go.

"Do you want me to find a place, or do you want to?"

She smiled. "Surprise me."

She turned and headed to the nursery, and he chuckled as he returned to his seat behind the desk. The emotions rumbling through him and his behavior were just silly, then he realized there was something different about her too. Probably the result of having made her decisions about school. Or maybe she'd found some grants and loans and some of her tension had eased?

Deciding that was probably it, he chose a restaurant in Bellagio, if only so they didn't have to waste too much time driving. The night was beautiful, and he had the top down on the convertible, but he had plans for when they returned. Maybe a moonlight swim.

They strolled to the restaurant and were immediately seated.

She looked around in awe. "It's so quaint."

He followed her lead, taking in the linen tablecloths, stone walls and shelves of wineglasses beside the wooden wine rack. "All the reviews say the food is wonderful."

She grinned. "I can't believe I'm here."

He took a menu from a waiter with a murmured, "Thank you," as her words settled in on him. That was what he should be feeling. A sort of disbelief that a woman from his past was suddenly in his present. But none of those emotions ever struck him.

That was what the *normal* feeling had been about. He'd always been comfortable with her. Which was probably why it had been so easy for him to ask her to join them as Darcy's nanny.

They ordered wine and the waiter left them to look over the menu. He saw a few things that intrigued him, but he couldn't stop thinking about how comfortable he was with her. How his schedule and his life would go back to the madness he hated when they returned to Manhattan.

And she'd go back to trouble.

He bit his bottom lip, then glanced over his menu at her. "Has it ever crossed your mind that maybe you should continue as my nanny when we return to Manhattan?"

She blinked, so surprised her expression froze comically.

He gaped at her. "It *never* crossed your mind?"

"When I think of going back, I keep seeing myself homeless."

He laughed. The waiter returned with their wine, plus a basket of warm bread and a plate of olive oil. They ordered their dinners and the waiter left again.

"You think it's funny that I'm going to be homeless?"

"No. I think it's awful. And I will *never* let

that happen. But I also can't believe that it never dawned on us that you could be Darcy's nanny while you're finishing your education. I think the easiest thing to do would be night school. You could study while Darcy was napping, and on nights that I couldn't get home in time for you to go to classes we could hire a sitter." He sniffed a laugh. "Nosey Cade has found two services that will provide fill-in nannies. Our schedules would run like clockwork."

She took a breath as she reached for her wine-glass. He expected her to gasp with happiness. Instead, she frowned.

"You don't agree?"

She sighed. "Wyatt. I like you guys. But you aren't my life. You're like the fairytale where the poor wench meets a prince who rescues her and then the book ends. Everybody thinks it's a happy ending but in real life, the wench goes back to sweeping the hearth and scrounging for grain to bake bread because that's who she is."

"That doesn't have to be true. Not with a job offer on the table."

She shook her head. "No. These two weeks were a break. A much-needed break for me to get my head on straight. But it's not my reality."

He hated the punch-in-the-gut feeling he got from her words. Part of him wanted to argue. The other part had no idea what his argument was. She was an intelligent woman who needed to get an education and move on. She was right. He and Darcy weren't her reality.

So why the hell did that make him feel awful?

Because working for him as Darcy's nanny could make the next year easy for her. Plus, her working for him solved a problem for them both. Yet she discounted it without thinking it through.

"I understand what you're saying, but I still need a nanny and even if you don't want to be with us forever, working for me for a year might be the answer to how you get your degree."

She played with her wineglass. "Maybe."

"No maybe about it. I am offering you the job."

"And I don't think it's the right choice for me."

Her tone of voice said the conversation was over and the waiter picked that precise moment to deliver their food.

Wyatt whipped his linen napkin off the table, not sure why he was so angry when she was an adult who had the right to make her own choices, but he was.

Her love of her dinner softened his annoyance. The way she took his hand as they walked to the convertible melted it a bit more. The moonlight drive, with her leaning across the seat to snuggle into him completely obliterated it.

As they got out of the car and exited the garage, he said, "So, how about a swim?"

"Now? It's midnight…" She glanced at her watch. "No, wait. It's only eleven."

At the bottom of the steps in the foyer, he laughed and pulled her to him. "If it's time you're worried about, we can undress as we race to the pool."

Her smiled grew. "And skinny dip."

"It's the best way to do what I have planned for us in the water."

She laughed.

"There you are!"

The sound of his father's voice coming from the living room sent a lightning bolt of confusion and revulsion down his spine.

Stretching to see beyond the foyer, he moved away from Sophie. "Dad?"

"And me too." His mother entered the foyer, glass of brandy in hand. "You are in so much trouble!"

"If it's curfew you're worried about Sophie just told me it's only eleven," Wyatt quipped.

"Don't screw off with us, Wyatt!" His dad's angry voice sent another chill down his spine. "It takes a maid to tell us we have a grandchild?"

CHAPTER ELEVEN

Wide-eyed, Sophie shifted around Wyatt. "I think I'll head up to my room."

An odd sensation shuffled through him as he watched her climb the stairs. He'd be racing away himself if these weren't his parents. But it somehow felt significant that she'd gone. That she hadn't stayed even long enough for him to introduce her to his parents.

"And who is that?" Wyatt's dad waved his hand indignantly at Sophie who had reached the top of the stairs. "Some floozie you dragged along on your fancy trip to Lake Como?"

"That's Darcy's nanny," Wyatt replied, so angry he could have spit fire. He eyed them suspiciously. His short, thin mom had brown hair cut in a blunt line. His dad was tall and thin with the same dark hair Wyatt had. Both were dressed as if they'd just come from the yacht club. "What are you doing here?"

"We heard you were here and wanted to surprise you," his mom said before taking a sip of brandy. "Guess we're the ones who got a surprise and not a good one."

Wyatt gaped at her. That was just like his parents. They never considered anyone but themselves. "Did you ever stop to think that if you'd let me know you were coming there wouldn't have been a surprise?"

His dad huffed out a sigh and headed to the living room. "I don't get it. I have absolutely no idea how we could have ended up with such an ungrateful son."

"I'm not ungrateful." The sting of being reprimanded hit first, but it was quickly followed by the knowledge that they didn't know him at all. They didn't see his successes. They didn't see his struggles. All they saw were their needs. He never spoke unkindly about them in public. He also gave his dad credit for pointing him in the direction of investing. He might not be the best son, but he was the kind of son they'd raised him to be. Quiet. Distanced. Available for their functions and always polite.

He was who they wanted him to be.

And the first time he didn't do exactly what they thought he should do, they were angry? No. He was not allowing that.

Wyatt followed his parents into the living room and walked directly to the bar where he poured himself a bourbon. The word *ungrateful* rattled through him. Still, he had a choice. Take a stand right now or say and do what he had to do to avoid arguments. After all, nothing he said or did would change them. Fighting would only make everyone uncomfortable. He chose the avoiding arguments route.

"You educated me and now I am self-sufficient."

"It would just be nice to see you now and again," his mom said, sitting on the sofa.

"You do see me at all your charity events."

His mom said, "Hmmm," as if she agreed.

His dad jumped right over that and went for the jugular, as he plopped down on the sofa beside his mother. "You kept a baby from us!"

He would have kept Darcy away from their toxicity forever if he could. He didn't want her paraded around Manhattan as their granddaughter and ignored at holidays. He didn't want her confused by an overabundance of attention one minute and absolutely no contact for weeks. He knew what it was like to be a child longing for affection and being ignored. He hadn't quite figured out how to protect his little girl, how to shield her, but he would. Right now, though, he stuck with facts, giving them the information his father wanted.

"I got her a few months ago from an old…girlfriend. We'd broken up over a year ago. I had no idea she'd gotten pregnant. But when she found out, I don't think she intended to tell me. I got the feeling she was enamored with the idea of being a mother. Then a job opportunity came up for her, and she suddenly didn't want to be a mom anymore. Her career came first. And I stepped up."

Horrified, his mom said, "You make her sound like a one-night stand! You got a baby from a one-night stand?"

"No. We dated a little longer."

"Fine. What kind of woman is she? Does she come from a good family? Good Lord, Wyatt? Do you even know anything about your child's background?"

His dad gaped at him. "Does she want money? Is she suing you? Is that what this is all about? She got pregnant to get at your money?"

"Dad, at this point I wouldn't care. I have custody and I also have lawyers. On top of that, I have a pretty strong case to keep custody, as Darcy's mom abandoned her."

"You've checked into it?"

He sat back in his chair. "A bit. But I've kept better tabs on Shelly. She's setting the world on fire and very happy in her job. After what she told me when she dropped Darcy in my lap, she's not coming back. If she does, I will deal with her."

His dad took a breath. "Have your lawyer draw up an agreement where she gives up her rights to the baby. Take it to her and make sure she signs it."

"No! I'm not having her give up her rights. At some point, Darcy might want a relationship—"

His mother groaned. "Are you insane? She sounds like trouble and the best way to head off trouble is nip it in the bud. Get that agreement signed now!"

"And never let Darcy know her mom?"

"She'll be better off for it."

"I disagree."

His father shook his head in disgust. "Just as I thought, you can't handle this."

"Actually, I can and I am. If you knew me better, you would realize no one pushes me around." Not even them. Not anymore.

Watching the amber liquid in her glass, his mother let out a disgusted breath. "I'm not sure how we'll introduce your child to society."

"You won't, Mom. I don't intend to raise her that way."

"Oh, Wyatt. Don't be ridiculous. She might be less than a year old, but she's *our* grandchild. Not only will the world want to see her, but there are some things we should be doing. Most parents get their children on waiting lists for the good schools before the baby's even born. If you haven't done that, I'd be happy to."

"I might home school her," Wyatt said. He'd always known this would be the real fight of his life. Giving his daughter a happier, healthier environment than the one he'd lived in. He hadn't realized it would start so soon. "Plus, Manhattan isn't the only place that has good schools. Or the only place I'm considering living."

His mother's horrified expression returned. "You might *leave* New York?"

"Cade owns an island. It might be nice to build a house there."

She flopped back on the sofa.

His dad stared at him. "You've spent years *building* a career—"

"And I have enough money that if I chose not to work ever again, I wouldn't have to." Maybe this was why he and Bonetti couldn't seem to get down to business about transferring ownership of his company? Maybe he wasn't supposed to throw himself into another project now? Maybe he would need all his energy to shield his daughter from his parents' need to run her life, to turn her into the perfect little princess who wouldn't really have friends because everyone was competition?

Not ready to get into that argument, he rose

from his seat. "It was a long day for me, and I have another long day tomorrow. If you don't mind, I'm going to bed."

He turned to leave but spun around again. "I'm assuming Mrs. P. got you settled in."

"She did."

"Goodnight, then."

After leaving Wyatt in the foyer with his parents, Sophie went to the nursery and checked on the baby then began walking across the room to the connecting door to her suite. It had taken heavy-duty self-discipline not to listen to the conversation taking place as she'd climbed the steps, but she hadn't. She wasn't part of this. After only a little over a week of working as Darcy's nanny, she had no right in a discussion with Wyatt's parents about their granddaughter.

She hesitated by the door to her bedroom. She'd spent the night before in Wyatt's room and they'd more than made plans to sleep together that evening. But with his parents' arrival those plans had gone out the window.

She opened the door to her room. It was better for her to be beside the nursery anyway. Not only was she closer to the baby but she didn't have clothes in Wyatt's room.

She tried to tell herself that the change of plans didn't matter, but the hollow feeling she'd had at her father's home the last year she'd lived there formed in her chest. At the time, she'd thought it was simply her eighteen-year-old self, longing to be out on her own. Now, she knew the urge to leave, to find her place, had been more about being an outsider looking in. Her father had a new wife, new kids, a whole new life and for the two years she'd lived with them, she'd been like a fifth wheel.

Just like she felt now.

She stopped those thoughts as she washed her face, brushed her teeth and slipped into her favorite silky pajamas because the empty feeling of having no one, belonging nowhere, filled her chest again. She stopped it by reminding herself that this was her time with Wyatt. Time to make memories. Time to relax and have some fun before she went home and faced God knew what. Having his parents arrive suddenly would certainly put a damper on that. But knowing Wyatt, he'd figure out a way for them to be together.

Focusing on that was much better than dwelling on the fact that she didn't really have a place in Wyatt's life, either.

Turning off the bedside lamp, she remembered Wyatt suggesting that she take the job as his nanny when they got home and for a few seconds she considered it, but she had to reject it. Their attraction was too powerful. They'd never have a simple working relationship. She would be a nanny having an affair with her charge's father. She'd be a cliché, but, worse, there were bigger things to consider. She liked him and Darcy so much that if she stayed a year, got accustomed to being in their lives that way, she'd probably never move on. There'd always be a reason to stay.

As his nanny.

Deep down inside she knew Wyatt didn't want her permanently. He liked being mobile. Being free. Plus, he was a guy who went after what he wanted. If he wanted her in his life forever, she'd know. He wouldn't have asked her to stay on as Darcy's nanny while she finished school.

Didn't matter. She would get her education, get a fabulous job and become someone. She wouldn't find her place. She would *make* her place.

She couldn't forget that.

Her bedroom door opened suddenly, and Wyatt walked in. "Can you believe them?"

Sophie only stared at him. He hadn't knocked. He entered as if he'd done it a million times before.

"Seriously, my mom's talking about schools already. Discussions about horseback riding lessons and competitions aren't far behind."

Realizing he needed a sounding board, someone to talk this out with, she raised herself to her elbows. "And that's bad?"

"Oh, dear God," he said, yanking off his shirt, then moving on to his belt.

She blinked. That was a little more than sounding board material.

"They ran my life like two drill instructors. I didn't have friends. Everybody was a potential competitor. And I didn't even have my parents. I saw them once or twice a week when my dad would grill me about my grades and my mother would remind me she would be mortified if I embarrassed her. It wasn't merely a lonely way to grow up. It was confusing." Without hesitation or question, he crawled into bed with her. "And now they want Darcy."

She almost said, "You'll figure it out," but he hadn't reached for her to make love. Instead, he lay beside her, his arms behind his head, on the pillow. His behavior was so casual, they could have been an old married couple or longtime lovers.

"You are Darcy's dad. You don't have to let them run her life."

"I know. I'm just furious that I have to keep them in line." He groaned. "They're horrible people. No. I should take that back. They aren't horrible. They're just not real. They live for what other people think and they never, ever considered my needs. Actually, most of the time I felt they never considered me a person. I was more like a possession that came with responsibility. After I got old enough to realize that, I also saw I wasn't the problem. They were. And that was a relief." He paused for a second. "But it's a lonely way to live."

Their parental troubles might be different, but the result was the same. Both she and Wyatt had had lonely childhoods. "Tell me about it."

He turned his head on the pillow to look at her. "I know. Your dad left you alone a lot too."

The fact that he remembered and understood filled her with happiness. But she wouldn't let herself make too much of it. She'd promised him this time to enjoy themselves while they were in Italy, but in moments like this she had to wonder how she could keep that promise without getting her heart broken. They always seemed so perfect together.

"My dad had no choice. He was working two jobs. Couldn't afford a sitter."

"Yeah."

The room grew quiet again. They were talking about loneliness—she'd been thinking about loneliness before he'd come into the room—but his opening up to her wrapped her in a warm, fuzzy feeling.

She squeezed her eyes shut, half letting herself bask in it and half reminding herself that this wasn't permanent.

But at least now she understood why he had so much trouble connecting to people. He'd never really been taught to make friends. He'd never experienced love or acceptance from his parents. He'd had to leave home to find reality.

He rolled over to kiss her goodnight and as he pulled away she smiled up at him.

He chuckled softly. "How can I feel better when my parents are still in the living room?"

She could have told him that their connection was as good for him as it was for her. But that was a Pandora's box best left closed.

"I don't know. Maybe out of sight, out of mind?"

He rolled his eyes. "I wish."

She walked her fingers up his chest. "I know a way we can take your mind off them."

He laughed, but he kissed her again. "We're supposed to be skinny dipping right now."

She shrugged. "I like it here." She smiled at him again. "We might want to consider checking to see if the door has a lock though. Your dad seems to enjoy barging in on people."

He snorted, but he locked the door before he returned to bed and made love like a guy who enjoyed her so much, he could never get enough of her.

But she'd already reasoned all of this out in her head. If he really couldn't get enough of her, he wouldn't have asked her to remain on as his nanny. He'd think of her very, very differently.

The next morning, Darcy woke them, and they simultaneously rolled out of bed and stumbled into the nursery.

Sophie found clothes for the baby while Wyatt changed her diaper. Then he brought Darcy into Sophie's room while she quickly dressed in something suitable for breakfast. Then they all went to his room.

He sat Darcy on the bed. "You know, you could take her to the dining room and get the breakfast ball rolling."

"Not on your life." She swung Darcy off his bed and to her hip. "I'm not risking saying the wrong thing to your parents."

In fact, she didn't intend to speak at all.

He laughed, wrestled a T-shirt over his head then took Darcy from Sophie before they went to the dining room together.

His parents were already eating. His dad quickly rose and pulled out a chair for Sophie.

"Thank you."

Wyatt slid Darcy into the highchair. "Mom, Dad, I didn't introduce Sophie to you last night. She's Darcy's nanny."

Sophie smiled at the petite woman with a sleek brown bob, wearing white pants and a sleeveless red top, and the tall, slender man with dark hair, wearing blue jeans that looked to have been ironed if the crisp crease was anything to go by. "How do you do."

"Sophie, my mom and Dad are Connie and Bruce."

Both nodded in acknowledgement, as Wyatt took his seat at the head of the table.

Mrs. P. arrived and Wyatt asked her to make Darcy whatever fruit and cereal she thought appropriate. Then he asked for eggs and bacon before he nodded to Sophie.

"I'd like my usual fruit platter."

"With cinnamon toast," Mrs. P. said with a sidelong glance at Wyatt's parents.

Stifling a laugh, Sophie said, "Sure."

Wyatt busied himself pouring coffee for himself and Sophie, then refilling his parents' cups. She knew he'd done it to avoid real conversation, but she also sensed that dichotomy again. He was part of their lives. He hadn't rebelled and shouted that he never wanted to see them again and disowned them. But he also wasn't *part* of their lives. He was cool. Rigid. And very much in control.

Mrs. P. arrived with Darcy's food first and Wyatt fed her. When his food and Sophie's arrived, he gave the baby a toy to play with while they ate. His parents stayed around for light conversation about the weather and their flight to Italy, and though on the surface it seemed perfectly normal, Sophie felt the undercurrent of Wyatt's distance.

"I can't wait to sightsee today," his mom said buoyantly. "You'll come with us, won't you, Wyatt?"

"We've actually been into town a few times," Wyatt began, but his father interrupted him.

"Good! That means we'll have a tour guide."

Cool and emotionless, Wyatt said, "Sure."

Because it was already after nine o'clock, Sophie saw herself with the rest of the morning and a few hours in the afternoon to look for loans and grants. She took Darcy upstairs, packed a diaper bag and waved goodbye when the cool, composed family headed into town.

But three hours later she heard the sound of the SUV returning. She almost stayed in her room and pretended she didn't hear them but realized that they'd probably come home because Darcy hadn't napped in the stroller as she usually did, and she was fussy.

She raced downstairs and met them in the foyer, where she took Darcy's carrier from Wyatt. "Let me guess. She needs a nap. Right?"

"Among other things," Wyatt said, heading for the bar in the living room.

Happy to scurry away, Sophie took Darcy upstairs, fed her a bottle and changed her into pajamas for her nap.

Walking to her room and her laptop to go back to investigating her future, she heard Wyatt and his parents talking though she couldn't quite make out what they were saying. Curiosity overwhelmed her and she tiptoed to the top of the stairs and quietly sat.

Wyatt's dad was half arguing, half whining. "I'm not saying we didn't like Bellagio. I'm just not one to walk around and look at things. We should have taken out the boat."

"Yes," Wyatt's mom agreed with her husband. "The boat would have been better."

So they hadn't come home to put Darcy down for a nap but because his parents had been bored—

In beautiful Bellagio?

Wow. Who gets bored in one of the most beautiful towns in the world?

The conversation stopped, then his mom said, "I'm going upstairs to check on the baby."

Sophie scrambled to her feet. She ran to her room, but not wanting Wyatt's mom to wake Darcy, she changed her mind, walked past her bed and slipped into the nursery. She was rifling through the little laundry basket, sorting clothes that needed to be washed by laying them out in several piles on the changing table, when his mom stepped inside.

"Oh, Sophie, you're here."

Sophie made a shushing motion with a finger to her lips.

His mom lowered her voice. "Sorry."

"It's okay," Sophie whispered. "Once she's sleeping you can talk. She just needs a few minutes to fall into a deep sleep."

As Sophie said that, Connie walked to the crib. She watched Darcy for a few seconds, while Sophie continued to sort through Darcy's dirty clothes.

Then finally she said, "I never thought I'd be a grandmother."

Sophie laughed softly. "The lament of all parents."

She strolled to the crib, standing beside Wyatt's mom. When she saw Darcy was in a deep sleep, she didn't stop Connie when she continued the conversation.

"Wyatt's always been so busy with his work, that we were fairly certain he wouldn't find a wife." She smiled at Sophie. "Now he doesn't have to."

Sophie conceded that with a nod, though a weird feeling tiptoed through her. Wyatt's mom didn't know Sophie was sleeping with her son. She was only talking about having a grandchild. But the sense of being an outsider again tightened her chest, hinting that she'd made a mistake sleeping with Wyatt.

But just hinting.

Just enough that she recognized the feeling.

Still, the sensation was incorrect. She hadn't made a mistake. She'd known what she was getting into. She wouldn't see Wyatt again once they returned to Manhattan. She'd miss him. She'd miss Darcy. But when she went home, she had a life to straighten out. She'd need space to get her act together. The memories of this time in Italy would bolster her.

"Anyway, now that we have a grandchild, I intend to see that she's raised properly."

That was exactly what Wyatt wanted to avoid—and she understood why. They seemed to have had an "on call" relationship with Wyatt. As a child, he'd been left alone and felt abandoned. He also felt pressured to be the best if his comment about friends being competition was anything to go by.

"Wyatt doesn't know a damned thing about good schools, dance lessons and getting a child on the right track for success."

That was so far off the mark that Sophie defended him without thinking. "He made a success of himself. I'm pretty sure he'll be a good dad."

Connie White turned from the crib, her eyes bright with anger. "Excuse me?"

Sophie gulped. She shouldn't have said anything, but defending Wyatt came so naturally she doubted she would have been able to hold back.

Besides, she'd only spoken the truth. She wouldn't apologize for that.

"I believe my husband and I had a hand in his success. We are the ones who raised him."

Oh, Lord. His mother was ridiculously clueless. But despite the urges she'd had to defend Wyatt, it wasn't Sophie's place to correct his mother.

Maybe an apology was in order after all?

"I'm sorry. That just slipped out."

Connie's eyes narrowed. "See that nothing like that slips out again." She straightened regally. "I don't care how long you've worked for Wyatt. Another slip gets you fired." She turned to the crib to look at her granddaughter, but quickly faced Sophie again. "Or if you really wanted to be a good nanny to this little girl, you'd get on board with making sure she has the suitable training."

For three seconds, Sophie was glad she wasn't Darcy's permanent nanny, then a hundred possibilities cascaded through her brain, things Connie could do if Wyatt hired a malleable caregiver for his daughter. Sophie could see Wyatt's mom turning Darcy's nanny into a spy. Or, worse, using her to take Darcy to schools or events that Wyatt hadn't approved. Now that Wyatt's mother was in Darcy's life, he'd have to be more careful than ever about whom he chose.

"I'm sure you have friends, connections," Connie said, holding Sophie's gaze. "Perhaps someone from your agency could help us get Darcy into the correct preschool."

"She's not even a year old yet."

"And if you're any kind of nanny at all, you know there are waiting lists to get into those academies." She studied Sophie. "Of course, you know that." She smiled stiffly. "You're sticking with Wyatt's side of things like a good nanny. But good nannies don't always listen to their boss. They think ahead." Her smile turned brittle. "Remember that." She headed to the nursery door. "And straighten up this room. It looks like a pigpen."

She nearly told Connie that she was sorting things to prepare to do laundry but bit her tongue. The less dealings she had with Wyatt's mom, the better. Plus, this was Wyatt's fight.

She stopped sorting as more pieces of Wyatt's puzzle fell together. He might have had trouble connecting with reality because he'd never seen it, but his parents were bullies. She'd watched Wyatt handle them by placating them half the time and standing up to them the other half. But she also recognized how difficult it must have been to break away, to create his own life—

And why he believed he had to keep them out of it. If he gave them an inch, they would take a mile.

But with a baby? Someone for Connie to spoil and show off? The comfortable life he'd built for himself was about to implode. There was no way Connie would stay out of her granddaughter's life, and once she squeezed in she would take over—

That had been his entire life. Not love. Not acceptance or encouragement. Demands until he erected walls and barriers.

It was no wonder he didn't believe in love, trust love. The people destined to be his first teachers hadn't ever shown him love. He'd spent his entire life battling for his sanity and freedom.

That's why he was so sure he'd never want to marry. Love had only ever hurt him, imprisoned him.

CHAPTER TWELVE

As HIS PARENTS took cocktails to the patio, Wyatt raced to the office to call Signor Bonetti. The older man almost sounded relieved when Wyatt explained that his parents had arrived unexpectedly, and he was showing them around.

"Go! Have fun! Let me know when they leave."

"No. I'll contact you as soon as I can. I don't have to hold their hands. Just entertain them a bit."

Disconnecting the call, he took a breath and leaned back in the leather office chair. He closed his eyes and released all the tension that had accumulated that morning while sightseeing. He could legitimately stay in the office for fifteen minutes, pretending the call had gone on longer, before he had to go outside and sit with his parents. He should enjoy them.

But he couldn't. He had to think this through. He knew what would happen now that they knew about Darcy. There'd be phone calls, a barrage of things he "had to" do and people he had to meet. His daughter wouldn't be a baby to them or even a person. She would be an item on a to do list. Someone they had to control to protect their image.

The way he saw it, they had now become the people *he had to control* to protect his daughter. But controlling them was never easy. They were strong and committed to the life they'd created. If he really wanted to protect Darcy, he would have to get her away from them.

Suddenly, the house on Cade's island didn't seem like a pipe dream. It felt like an escape.

But wasn't it a shame he had to run away to protect his child?

A knock on the office door had him opening his eyes. Seeing Sophie, he smiled. "What's up?"

"Your mother is a piece of work."

He laughed. "No kidding. I was just realizing that if I want to protect Darcy, I'll probably have to build a house on Cade's island and home school her."

"You can't do that." She walked into the office and gingerly sat on the chair across from his desk. "She'll need friends, socialization."

He remembered being alone most of his childhood, until he was a teenager and able to make some of his own choices. It had been his first taste of the real world. University, though, was where he really grew enough to see that his parents' lives were cold and sometimes cruel.

Not what he wanted. Certainly not what he wanted for Darcy.

"You're right." He pulled in a breath. "There are actually a few families in the Montgomery."

"Readymade friends," Sophie said with a laugh. "But that's not to say you shouldn't build a *vacation* house on Cade's island." She frowned. "Unless, of course, there are enough rooms in Cade's retreat that even if he and Trace are already there, you and Darcy could still have a room. I imagine spending long weekends there with friends is really fun."

Damned if she wasn't right again.

"In twenty seconds, you've totally talked me out of building a house."

"I guess I have."

"I'm still going to have trouble with my parents if I stay in Manhattan."

"You can keep your distance."

He shook his head. "No. If you think that, you don't understand. My parents are like dogs with a bone. I broke away. But Darcy's fragile."

"Not fragile, just vulnerable. The best way to protect her is with the stability of a permanent home."

"I had a home in Manhattan my entire life, and all the markings of stability. It didn't help with parents who monitored my every move and scheduled my life into infinity, while barely having any contact with me aside from the few times they would order me downstairs and browbeat me on my schoolwork or scold me about embarrassing them." He took a breath. "No. A permanent home didn't help."

"Okay, if that's true, then the reverse should be true."

He eyed her as if she were crazy. "What?"

"If Darcy had people in her life who loved her, she would be fine wherever she lived."

"You would think that would be true."

"It will be if you set lines and limits for your parents."

"It's not going to be easy. They'll sneak in while I'm at work, probably bribe the nanny to report on my comings and goings."

Her face shifted. Her happy expression disappeared, and she quickly looked down at her hands. After a few seconds, she looked back up at him again. "Your mom already approached me about some of that."

He gaped at her. "What?"

"She mentioned that if I wanted to be a good nanny, I should help her do the things she wants to do with the baby. Like, get her into the best school."

He closed his eyes and sighed. "She's only known she has a grandchild for twenty-four hours and already she's undermining me. This is going to make finding a new nanny doubly hard."

Sophie caught his gaze. "What if I stayed on as Darcy's nanny… At least until I finished school."

His breathing froze. "When I suggested that you said no."

"I changed my mind. Your mom is formidable. In this year, while you're establishing the ground rules for how your parents are allowed in Darcy's life, I'll stay. I'll help. You know she can't bribe me or threaten me. I'm not afraid of her."

Even though her suggestion shocked him, he could feel a smile forming, and relief pour through him. "Really?"

Before Sophie could answer, his phone rang. He picked it up and rolled his eyes heavenward. "It's my dad." He turned toward the big office window that showcased the pool and waved at his father.

"He called you?"

His phone rang again. "Either they want me outside to entertain them or they need their drinks refilled."

She rose. "I'll do it."

"No." He couldn't have been more emphatic. "If you're staying on as Darcy's nanny for the year while you're in school, I don't want them deciding you are the maid." He rose from his chair. "Stick to your duties."

He started out of the office but stopped by Sophie's chair, leaned down and kissed her. "Thank you."

That night, Sophie declined dinner with his parents. Wyatt said he was taking them to the little restaurant they'd found in Bellagio, and she suggested she stay home and care for the baby.

He didn't seem happy about her decision, but he was the one who had told her to make sure she kept her job duties clear. As much as that meant she couldn't slip over into maid duties, it also meant not hanging out as if she was part of the family.

He and his parents left without her, and she and Darcy had a good time, waltzing through the house until it was time to get her ready for bed.

The baby fell asleep immediately, and though Sophie had some applications to fill out, she stayed in the nursery a few minutes longer than necessary trying to get adjusted to the fact that she'd agreed to be Darcy's nanny for a year.

It was going to be hard.

So hard. Not only would she not split with

Wyatt when she returned to Manhattan and regain her bearings, but also she'd have another year of falling in love with both him and Darcy.

She'd be a cliché.

She'd get her heart broken.

But when she looked into the crib, at sleeping Darcy, she knew exactly why she had done it. Wyatt might be excellent at thinking things through, but he also had the money and connections to make spur of the moment decisions that wouldn't be right for Darcy.

She couldn't live on an island with no friends and no influence except adults. She had to be around people her own age. She had to have experiences with other kids.

And like it or not, she needed contact with her grandparents.

Just very careful contact.

She tucked a cover over Darcy's tiny form and turned away from the crib. She would sacrifice a year.

Not just a year. Her heart.

She was going to have one hell of a broken heart when she graduated university and moved on.

But she *would* move on. That was a promise she was making to herself. When her schooling was done, no matter what the situation with Wyatt, she would move on.

Wyatt and his parents returned a little after ten o'clock. She saw the car drive up to the house and turned off her light immediately to discourage Wyatt from coming to her room.

Ten minutes later the door opened and though she kept her eyes closed, he slipped out of his clothes and crawled into bed with her.

She turned toward him.

"I hope I didn't wake you."

"No. I hadn't even really started to drift off."

"Worried about your decision to stay on as nanny?"

It could have impressed her that he was concerned about her, but she knew he was a considerate man, a man who saw all angles of everything. Though the question showed his innate kindness, she didn't take it as anything more than it was.

"No. You need me. Darcy needs me. I'll have somewhere to live while I finish school. It's win-win."

He chuckled. "I told you that yesterday."

She could have argued that there were lots of things he wasn't taking into consideration, like her broken heart, but that was her cross to bear. "How was your night?"

"My parents hated that we had to walk to the restaurant from the parking area, loved the restaurant and griped about the walk again."

She laughed.

He said nothing for a few seconds, then he shook his head. "They're snooty and condescending but, in a way, that makes their behavior very predictable."

"Which should give us the ability to stay one step ahead of them."

He said, "I have for the past twelve years," then snuggled against her. "Knowing Darcy's caregiver is on my side, I can protect her."

He said nothing for a few minutes. She let the silence linger in case he wanted to talk some more but soon she heard the deep, even sound of his breathing. The day had been difficult, and she knew he needed the rest.

She turned on her pillow with a satisfied smile, happy he was relieved she'd decided to take the job as his nanny for a year, and content that she could do this for both him and Darcy. She could make that sacrifice.

Then the weirdest thought hit her.

What if this was real love? Not just romantic love. But deep, abiding love.

Sacrificing for him and Darcy, letting him talk, letting him fall asleep naturally. All that was real love. He needed her as more than a nanny. He just plain needed her. But as long as things were running smoothly, she didn't think he would realize it.

The sound of the baby fussing came through the monitor speaker, and she rolled out of bed and headed for the nursery.

Wyatt was right behind her.

Seeing Darcy's diaper needed changing, she removed it and Wyatt handed her a dry one. Then she put the baby in the crib again and rubbed her tummy until she fell asleep and she and Wyatt tiptoed back to bed.

But as they both slid under the covers, she realized that they were forming a family. They talked about issues. They both cared for Wyatt's little girl. They both wanted what was best for her. And Wyatt didn't make her feel as if she was giving an opinion when they talked about Darcy. They made decisions together. Like equals. Like *parents*.

It felt like a family to her.

But no matter how much they talked, how much they drew conclusions and worked things out, they weren't forming anything permanent. Wyatt didn't want anything permanent, and she understood why. His clearest example of marriage and family wasn't a good one. Actually, he believed it was a bond to be fought against. He'd been fighting against it since he was eighteen. He'd fight it forever. And she refused to be the woman who thought she could change a man.

* * *

The next morning, Wyatt's parents finished their breakfast and announced that they were going to see the vineyards in Tuscany.

Sophie glanced up from her fruit and cinnamon toast.

"We've been there before, of course," Connie said with a laugh. "But it doesn't hurt to have another visit or two on your social résumé."

Sophie struggled to keep her eyebrows from raising at that.

"We've actually called a real estate agent to show us around," Wyatt's dad picked up the conversation. "We're considering buying a place there. All our friends are."

"I don't think we should," Connie said. "Every once in a while, it looks good to be the person who doesn't follow the crowd, right, Wyatt?"

This time, Sophie blinked. How his mother could compare the choice not to buy a villa with Wyatt's life choices was beyond her.

"Anyway," Bruce said, tossing his linen napkin to his plate and rising from his chair. "It will be worth a day out and about."

"With an appropriate tour guide," Connie said, as she too rose. "Not someone who will take us to common tourist attractions—"

Sophie almost winced at that, but Wyatt remained emotionless.

"Someone who knows what he's doing."

Out of politeness, Wyatt stood as his mom did. "I thought you were looking for a place to buy?"

"Maybe yes. Maybe no," Bruce said. "With the amount of money we would be spending if we did buy, the agent knows a day of showing us around is worth the gamble."

Wyatt simply said, "Well, enjoy yourselves."

His parents left the dining room and Wyatt took his seat again, sending her a smile.

She shook her head in response as he dug into the rest of his breakfast.

He didn't have to say a word. Neither did she. They acknowledged that his parents were a bit absurd with a few looks.

The thought almost made her laugh. She loved their connection and knew it would help as they dealt with his parents over the next year.

Everything felt like it was falling into place.

Wyatt finished his coffee, then said, "I talked with Signor Bonetti before breakfast. He told me to come over any time this morning."

"Okay."

Groaning, he stood up. "God knows when I'll be back." He leaned in and kissed her.

"Then I'll see you when I see you."

Later that morning, when Darcy was napping, Sophie found an email from Wyatt's staff with an attachment that was her statement for the media.

It was short, simple and perfect. Just a line she could toss over her shoulder to keep reporters at bay.

If she ever actually saw one. Going home with Wyatt, living in his penthouse, not signing a lease for another apartment, put her off the grid. She got the sudden, unwanted feeling that it could look like she was hiding. But she couldn't exactly call the media and tell them she hadn't rented an apartment because she'd taken a job as a nanny.

A nanny.

The word rattled through her. No matter how close she and Wyatt had become, no matter that it felt like they were forming a family, they weren't. Her primary place in his life was as Darcy's nanny, an employee. *She'd* made it official when she agreed to keep the job when they returned to Manhattan.

With her emotions jumbled, she didn't leave her room when she heard the sounds of Wyatt returning. Because he didn't come upstairs to check on Darcy or to change into swimwear, she figured he was still working.

She could go to the office and see what was going on, but her confused feelings had her walking to the door one second and turning away from it the next. A nanny wouldn't run downstairs to see what he was doing. A *girlfriend* would. But she wasn't really a girlfriend.

She was a nanny...with confidences?

She had no idea what she was. He'd talked to her about important things on this trip. When she was his girlfriend, he hadn't. They'd connected. They were caring for his daughter like parents... not people dating. Not a nanny and her boss.

Pacing her bedroom, she raked her fingers through her hair. She understood his feelings and fears about relationships. She also knew, absolutely knew, how easy it was for her to see more in their interactions than he intended—

That was why he'd broken up with her. She'd taken their romance as more than he intended. Right now, they had a sweet deal. He got a nanny. She got a place to live while she finished her degree. They also had each other.

It might not be forever, but the next year could either be happy or make her crazy with confusion.

She opted to be happy with her choices. After all, she was going to get her degree in this year too. If she kept her wits about her, this could be one of the happiest years of her life.

Still, part of her ached for more from their relationship. She'd never had a connection with anyone that was stronger. She'd already realized this was real love—

But what if it wasn't?

What if, like when they were dating three years ago, she was making more out of everything he said and did than what he meant?

She could not face that embarrassment again.

If there was more between them, he had to be the one to say it.

CHAPTER THIRTEEN

WYATT WALKED DIRECTLY into the office, closed the door and opened his laptop, immediately calling Trace and Cade.

Both said, "What's up?"

If Wyatt hadn't been in a mood, he might have laughed at how in sync they were. "I'm just back from what I think will be my last visit with Bonetti."

Trace winced. Cade laughed.

"It's not what either of you think. Last night Bonetti got a call from his daughter saying she and her family were going out on her yacht, sailing to Monaco, and they invited him along. So he gave me a little slip of paper." Wyatt waved it at the computer. "And he told me that's his price."

Trace sat up. "He gave you a number?"

"Yep." Wyatt read Bonetti's asking price to his friends.

Cade whistled.

Trace sat back in his seat. "He's had this number all along?"

"No. He said he based it on things we'd discussed. But he has conditions. He showed me a five-year plan a couple days ago. I told him we could not promise we would adhere to it. He wants his employees to keep their jobs. He also wants financial security for his family. If you think the number is high, that's why. He believes that number reflects the fact that we're not giving his family a percentage of the profits. So the purchase price needed to be higher."

Cade said, "Do we get a chance to counteroffer?"

"I'm guessing we can if we get it to him tonight. Tomorrow he's gone. If we're going to counteroffer, it has to be our best and final."

Trace said, "So what do you think?"

"I say we spend the afternoon running numbers."

They spent the rest of the day and part of the evening working up a counteroffer. Wyatt called Bonetti and after only a second's hesitation, he took the deal.

And just like that Wyatt was free.

He felt as if a burden had been lifted from his shoulders until he walked out of the office and heard the sounds of his parents in the living room.

Tired beyond belief, he headed to the living room anyway. "I just finished the deal with Signor Bonetti."

His dad said, "Fabulous. Let's have a drink to celebrate."

He ran his hand along the back of his neck. "Actually, Dad, I'm exhausted. I think I'm going to shower and go to bed."

Neither of his parents looked happy as he turned to walk out of the room, but he pivoted back again. "Did you find a vineyard or villa you liked?"

"Two." His dad winced. "But honestly I don't think we're made to live abroad."

"Okay. We'll see you in the morning."

He turned away again on a course for Sophie's room. He opened the door without knocking and found her leaning over her computer.

"What's up?"

"I got the statement from your PR department today."

"Oh, that's great." He walked over and slid his arms around her shoulders. "I bought a great big company today."

She turned in his arms. "You did?"

He grinned. "Yeah." He bent and kissed her. "What to join me in the shower?"

She hesitated. She tried to hide it, but he saw. Still, she said, "Sure."

She stood up and unbuttoned his shirt.

His eyebrows rose. "Are we getting a little ahead of ourselves here?"

"With a baby sleeping in the next room, it's always best to take advantage of the time."

He laughed, then realized there was no humor in her voice. For a second, he wondered if something was wrong with her. Especially when she reached up and kissed him, almost desperately. But desperation became a hot tango of lips and tongues as heat and need ignited his blood. Even thoughts of his parents in the living room didn't bother him. Everything was better now. He had his company. Sophie had agreed to be Darcy's nanny for a year.

He could not have asked for a better outcome to this trip.

He half kissed, half danced her into the bathroom connected to her bedroom. The place was smaller than the bath for the primary bedroom, but it was still comfortable and spa-like with a marble shower, gray floors and natural wood shelves for fluffy white towels and toiletries.

He yanked her T-shirt over her head, and she stepped out of her sweatpants. He grabbed a bottle of body wash as they entered the shower.

They stood under the spray, and he closed his

eyes and pretended they were outside, in a gentle storm, just the two of them happy and content.

He ran kisses down her neck and didn't protest when she slid her hands over his chest and back. There was something so perfect about being with her that he couldn't capture the feeling, except to know that when she was wet and naked against him nothing else in the world mattered.

He pressed her to the shower wall and sank into her, relishing the feeling, so glad she'd be with him for the next year that for once in his life he didn't have a care in the world.

CHAPTER FOURTEEN

THE NEXT MORNING, they left his parents in Italy to fend for themselves, and headed for the private airstrip to return to Manhattan. Their two weeks weren't up, but with the deal done, he needed to go home to set things up.

Though he'd never felt better, happier, more in control, he could see something was bothering Sophie. She'd been quiet at breakfast, quiet while they packed Darcy's things, quiet when they'd said goodbye to his parents. Now, getting ready to take off, he could see something in her eyes.

Her silence unexpectedly reminded him of the cold wars his parents had, but he told himself that was idiotic. There was absolutely nothing Sophie could be trying to get her way about by using the silent treatment. They'd made their deal like consensual adults. She'd gotten what she needed and he was getting what he needed.

When she buried herself in her book, he decided he had to be imagining things. And comparing her silence to the silence of his mother? He probably made that connection because he'd just spent two days with his parents.

Still exhausted from his long, confusing ten days of dealing with Bonetti and his parents, he fell asleep on the flight and woke when Sophie told him the pilot was getting ready to land. He snapped Darcy in her car seat and Sophie buckled in herself, perfectly normal behavior for two people with a baby.

A limo awaited them when they landed at another private air strip, this one close to New York City. Carrying Darcy, Wyatt led Sophie to their ride. They climbed inside and Wyatt buckled Darcy into a car seat.

As the limo pulled away from the private jet, Wyatt leaned back. "Well, here we go. I now have a new business to organize, and you need to get enrolled in school, while we both figure out a way to deal with my parents and you handle the fallout from your mother's embezzling."

Beside him on the bench seat, she sat oddly prim and proper.

She was never prim and proper. She knew when to be polite and dignified, but she never had the tight look of someone playing a role—

Unless she was upset? Or scared? She'd mentioned at least twice that returning to Manhattan was returning to trouble.

"Are you nervous?"

She jumped when he spoke. "Huh?"

He laughed. "I asked if you were nervous because of everything going on with your mom. Although," he drew the word out as he realized something. "If you don't rent an apartment or do anything public, you'll literally be hidden in my house."

She took a breath. "I thought of that yesterday."

"So this is good for you?" he asked, pointing back and forth between her and Darcy, wanting confirmation that she was okay.

She said nothing.

Her silence reminded him of his mom again. His dad always had to play twenty questions, trying to get her to talk.

But after a few more seconds, she took another long breath. "Yes. The arrangement is great."

Her answer should have relieved him, but confusion overwhelmed him. Never in their relationship had she behaved this way. He knew something was wrong, but she clearly didn't want to talk about it.

He settled back on his seat, rejecting a sliver of anger that tried to form. He understood that she didn't want to talk. He understood that she was nervous. He would let her alone to deal with her feelings.

The limo grew silent. The closer they got to the Montgomery, the more her expression tightened and the more worried he became.

"Sophie?"

She faced him. "What?"

"You know, you don't have to deal with whatever is bothering you alone. We can talk about anything."

Her head tilted. "Really? *Anything?*"

"Yes!"

She took a breath and blew it out slowly. "Okay, then I want to talk about us."

"Us?"

"What are we doing, Wyatt?"

Totally not comprehending, he looked at her. Right now, they were on their way to his house. She was going to be Darcy's nanny. He would help her with school. None of that should make her unhappy or confused or nervous.

"I'm not sure what you mean."

"When we're alone, we're lovers. When your parents were around, I was Darcy's nanny. For the past few days, I've felt like two people."

Once again, his parents' involvement had screwed things up. "That was to protect you."

"You're saying you'll be yourself when we're around Trace and Cade?"

He blinked. "Why would we be around Trace and Cade?"

"We're not going to go out? Ever?"

"Go out?"

"Are we dating again? Am I just your nanny? What are we doing?"

"I need you as my nanny. And you're the one who made it sound like you're unhappy with the *dating* aspect of our relationship."

"I feel like your dirty little secret."

Insult poured through him and he blinked. "What?"

"Think it through."

Her hesitation before making love the night before popped into his mind. He'd been correct that something was bothering her.

He tried seeing the situation through her eyes but didn't see what she obviously saw. They were friends. Or so he thought. They talked about everything. She was in on every decision they'd made.

"We never did or said anything that we didn't agree upon."

"That's true. But things changed while we were in Italy."

They'd talked. She'd agreed to stay on as Darcy's nanny for a year. Damn it! They *were* friends. "I thought things changed for the better."

"It was better."

"Until my parents came."

She winced. "That's part of it but not the whole

deal. Wyatt, you're missing a big piece of the picture. You're missing why you want me to stay on as Darcy's nanny and why I hated thinking of you returning to Manhattan without someone to help you with your parents."

"I thought that was because we were friends."

"We're more than friends. With time to ourselves and caring for Darcy together, our feelings for each other grew."

His breath stalled as he finally understood what she was saying. "You think we fell in love."

"You don't?"

His heartbeat slowed down then revved up as fear collided with disbelief. "No. I don't think we fell in love." He'd just spent two days with parents who epitomized everything he hated and wrapped it up in a package they called love. "The past two days you were with my parents. Honestly…is *that* what you want out of life?"

"Absolutely not. From what little I saw, your parents don't know how to love. But you do."

His heart stuttered to a stop. He didn't believe in love because he'd never seen it. He'd always acknowledged that. Now, Sophie was telling him he loved her? Memories of feelings he'd been unable to identify jumped into his brain. Feelings while they made love, while she cuddled Darcy, while they did simple, happy things.

What if he did love her?

No. He couldn't. A person could not "do" something they'd never seen let alone been taught.

It was much easier to believe all those emotions he'd felt were passing things. Hormones. Endorphins. Dopamine. Good moods that would dissipate over time and leave two people floundering to either protect what never really existed, the way his parents had, or hurt each other and move on.

He wouldn't inflict that on either one of them.

He pulled in a breath. "Look. We had a good time in Italy. We absolutely connected and we made plans that benefitted both of us. Don't turn that into something it isn't."

His words stung like the crack of a whip. They made Sophie feel small and stupid, but she wasn't letting him miss the bigger picture. "So, you'd rather take me back to Manhattan, install me in your house as Darcy's nanny, sleep with me, and raise Darcy together but never commit."

"Commit?" He gaped at her. "Is that what this is all about? You want a ring?" He laughed. "After what? Ten days together?"

She'd thought his last comment had hurt? A knife in her chest would have done less damage. Still, meeting his parents, seeing his life up close and personal, she understood why he was so resistant. Though she hadn't wanted to try to change him, she finally realized forcing him to recognize his feelings for her wasn't changing him. It was pointing out the obvious. Getting him to see reason. Setting out facts in a way that he could see what had happened between them.

If she had to fight to do that, she would fight.

"If we really break down everything you've said today, you're avoiding making a commitment because you don't believe ten days is long enough to trust me forever."

"I don't trust *anyone* forever."

"You trust Trace and Cade."

"As business partners. They stand to lose as much as I do. We have to trust each other. But that doesn't mean we'll be together forever. Business partners move on. I'd like to think we'll be friends for our entire lives. But I simply don't believe in fairytales."

The thought that he thought he and the two guys he considered to be like brothers might drift apart astounded her into silence.

"Sophie, listen to me. My parents raised me in the worst, most empty way, and if there is such a thing as love, I never saw it. I can't believe in something that's insubstantial at best. And, at worst, is a way for people to hurt each other."

She stared at him, suddenly feeling like it was three years ago. His arguments hadn't changed.

His beliefs hadn't changed. Even the way he behaved hadn't changed.

And she finally saw that he might have learned a thing or two from his parents after all. He could have created his beliefs to protect himself, but he did not seem to recognize that he was hurting her.

And if he did, protecting himself was more important to him.

The hurt was so deep, she wasn't sure she could move or speak. But she also saw he'd never led her on, always been up front with her. If there was blame to be placed it was on her.

He'd always told her the truth. She'd simply never understood it because to her it was so obvious they were good for each other.

And she'd loved him.

Familiar streets appeared around her. Even as her heart shattered into a million pieces, her brain righted itself. She'd fought for what she wanted, and she'd lost. She hated leaving Darcy, hated breaking a commitment, but there was a time in every person's life when they needed to face truth and act accordingly.

"Tell your driver to stop."

"We're two blocks away from the Montgomery."

"I know. I'm going to get a ride share and go

to my dad's." When he only looked at her, she said, "Tell the driver to stop."

His face registered his recognition of what she was really saying. She wasn't going home with him.

"Come up to the condo. We can talk about this some more."

"No. I love you. I really, honestly love you." The liberation of saying that rode through her. For once she got to say what she felt without worry. He'd already broken them apart. Her telling him she loved him made no difference, except to free her.

"You don't feel that for me. If I work for you for an entire year, it will kill me. I'm sorry about Darcy. I'm sorry I said I would be her nanny and now I'm bailing. But you know what? Lots of people have hurt me too. I always accept it, but this time I can't. For once I'm going to do what's right for me."

"All your suitcases are in the trunk of the limo."

"I'll get them tomorrow while you're at work. Leave them with Pete. Tell him I'll be by." When he only stared at her, she said, "Stop the car."

He did as she asked and she jumped out, reiterating that she'd get her things the next day. Then she closed the door on Wyatt White and his adorable daughter.

The sights, sounds and scents of Manhattan surrounded her. Tall buildings and people. Taxi horns. Hot dogs and bakeries.

None of this was hers anymore. She had to find an apartment she could afford, get a new job, and, hopefully, fit in her last year of university.

All with a broken heart.

Her fault this time.

Still, she was lost, alone, so empty she wasn't sure how she found the strength to stand.

The limo pulled into traffic again.

She'd made a mistake, a huge mistake in restarting their romance, because she now loved Wyatt. For real. In that earthy, honest, vulnerable way that causes a person to open their soul, sacrifice and share everything…

And he'd rejected her.

Getting over him this time was going to hurt much worse than the last heartbreak she'd gotten from him.

But she was stronger than she was three years ago. He might not believe in love, but she did. She knew love was out there and someday she'd find it.

It didn't stop the hurt of losing him, of losing something that could have been great. No one ever confided in her as he had, no one ever listened to her the way he had. They'd had a one-shot opportunity at perfection, and he hadn't wanted it.

Her soul ached at the thought, but she yanked the strap of her purse higher on her shoulder and started walking.

She'd call her ride share when she was sure she was done crying.

That night after putting Darcy to bed, Wyatt sat in his grand living room, with thoughts of Sophie getting out of the car haunting him.

Even though she'd been the one who promised to be Darcy's nanny for a year then bailed, he felt like he'd let her down.

He hadn't. He'd been up front with her from day one. Plus, three years ago he'd told her he didn't want a commitment. He didn't believe in love. He owed her nothing.

Except money for being Darcy's nanny in Italy and he had no idea where she was.

He could call her, but he got out his laptop and searched her dad's address and found it easily. He would take care of the money issue in the morning. Face to face. Fairly because he was fair.

Having a plan to fulfill his responsibilities to her should have eased his mind, but it didn't.

He tossed and turned in bed and woke grouchy. When he walked into the suite for Three Musketeers Holdings, Cade frowned but Trace strolled into the office and groaned when he saw Darcy in the carrier on Wyatt's chest.

"You told us you had a nanny."

"I did." He winced. "She quit."

Cade said, "No big surprise there." But accustomed to having Darcy around, he got down to the business of going over potential articles of agreement for the purchase of Signor Bonetti's business.

Wyatt stopped him once so he could feed Darcy and put her down for a nap in the play yard he kept in his office.

When he went back to work, neither Cade nor Trace said anything about the pause. As if they'd never stopped, they picked up the next article for the batch they'd be giving to their lawyers.

Trace said something about the financing schedule and Wyatt zoned out. He knew there was plenty of money. He didn't care if they dipped into their personal fortunes to buy something new. But Trace always liked knowing everybody was on the same page. So Wyatt let him ramble even if it did make him smile.

When he realized he was smiling, happy to be with his two friends, he remembered telling Sophie that he believed their partnership wouldn't last forever and maybe even their friendship would break down eventually.

It was foolish to think otherwise. Trace now

lived in Italy. He could decide to bow out of Three Musketeers at any time. So could Cade. He could choose to live the life of a reclusive island guy—

The thought tightened his chest. He didn't want to lose contact with either of his friends. He loved the women they'd chosen to marry...

And the thought that either one of them would marry and then divorce also made him feel funny.

He yanked his mind away from those things and focused on the articles they were drafting.

Darcy woke a few hours later and Trace suggested they call it a day. He'd brought Marcia to Manhattan to shop and, just like that, Wyatt could see Sophie showing Marcia around Manhattan, having fun with her.

He shoved those thoughts aside and followed his partners to the private elevator.

"You're welcome to have dinner with us tonight. I know Marcia would love to see you."

Wyatt glanced over at Trace with his glasses and ever-present smile. He pointed at Darcy. "Still no nanny, remember?"

"Yeah. How did you lose this one?"

Cade's question made Wyatt suck in a breath. He did not want to explain fully. He didn't feel comfortable embarrassing himself or Sophie that way.

"I thought we'd struck a deal for her to stay on once we returned from Italy. She had second thoughts and left."

"I know this has something to do with you," Cade badgered. "I mean, Trace and I see your goodness, but you can be gruff."

"I'm not gruff."

The elevator stopped in the basement parking garage.

"You are gruff," Trace said. "But we get it. You have a lot of responsibilities on your shoulders."

Glancing down to be sure Darcy was asleep, Wyatt said, "Thank you."

But for the first time he realized that he didn't do such a good job of hiding the pressure. He thought he was strong, above the normal feelings that usually plagued a leader, but they knew. They'd seen.

"Well, whatever your nanny's reasons for abandoning you, she must have been a gem because we've never seen you so calm."

Wyatt's breath stuttered. "She didn't abandon me." And she had pointed out that they were good for each other. At least twice. He'd heard. He'd agreed. But here in Manhattan with the two people he trusted the most in his life, those simple words carried more weight.

Or something.

Hours later, pacing the big main room of his penthouse, with the floor-to-ceiling view of the Upper East Side, he tried to get thoughts of Sophie, being happy with Sophie, out of his brain, but his nerve endings shivered with something he couldn't identify, and it made him crazy.

First of all, he'd hated that Trace thought Sophie had abandoned him. She wasn't like that. If anything, he'd pushed her. He could have placated her in that limo, but his need for protection drove him. Plus, he didn't want to get into something then hurt *her*. It was better to be the guy who didn't believe in love, than the guy who tried a real relationship and ended up hurting her even more with a bad marriage.

Second, he'd never worried about a former lover or girlfriend, but he couldn't stop thinking about Sophie. Not really worrying. She was a tough cookie. She'd taken him on a few times. After only ten days of being together, she would get over this quickly.

Wouldn't she? Of course, she would. But his heart expanded with pain as he envisioned her thinking their breakup was no big deal. That she'd move on and he'd never see her again. He'd never see her smile. Never hear her laugh. Never see her play with Darcy or have her play with him. No swimming. No pastries. No laughing at cinnamon toast.

Third, his parents kept tiptoeing into his brain. The idea that they deserved each other morphed into a realization that they'd made their choices. Whether it seemed lopsided to him or something like torture, it hadn't been his choice to make. It had been theirs.

He flopped onto the sofa but the whole idea of choices wouldn't let him go.

How people made choices and did things because that's what they wanted.

That edged over into the idea that he always thought of love in the negative. Always saw it as hormones, dopamine or wishful thinking. But if someone had something good—as he'd had with Sophie—it didn't matter if they called it hormones or love.

If they really wanted it to last, they could do things to assure it would last. They could make choices that took them and the relationship in the direction of stability and longevity.

This time when his chest tightened it was with the strangest feeling.

Hope.

The entire time he and Sophie were in Italy, he'd been happy. He knew that was because of Sophie. She'd always made him happy. But he wouldn't let himself tip over into acknowledging it or, worse, seeing what she'd seen, that they really had connected this time. That they'd done things for each other. That they enjoyed each other's company, shared their concerns, both wanted the best for the other.

He wouldn't because he'd been so sure he was right. That there was no such thing as love.

But what if he was wrong?

Even if love was dopamine, hormones and wishful thinking, a person had control over what they did and didn't do. A smart guy could make it last.

He frowned.

A smart guy *could* make it last. If he wanted loving her to last a lifetime, it would. He was a very determined man.

The thought made him laugh out loud.

He *was* a very determined guy. And he knew nothing in heaven or hell could stop him if he decided to make their love work—forever. No shelf life.

Under ordinary circumstances, he'd give himself a day or two to think this through. But his gut clenched and his chest tightened.

He'd let her leave the limo without so much as an argument. He'd let her think he didn't love her, didn't want her, was only upset that she was breaking her nanny commitment—

Realizing how much that would have hurt her, he fell back on the sofa.

He couldn't bear the way he'd hurt her.

* * *

Sophie took the pillow from her stepmom and fluffed it a bit before she set it on the pull-out sofa bed.

"If I forgot to tell you yesterday, thank you for letting me crash here."

Her stepmom sat on the arm of the oversize floral chair on which her dad sat in the basement family room of the house they'd recently remodeled.

"We tried to call you when we heard about your mom on the news, but the calls didn't go through."

"I was in Italy. I don't have an international phone plan."

Her dad laughed. "I'm still not sure I understand that whole thing with Wyatt."

"He needed a nanny while he was in Italy. I needed to get out of town to think things through. It was perfect timing."

"Isn't he an old boyfriend though?"

"Yes," Sophie said, working not to wince. "But he was negotiating most of the time we were there." She didn't tell them about the romantic sightseeing trips or the boat ride with Darcy or swimming. "That's why he needed me. He also had his staff write me a really good 'no comment' statement for the media."

Her stepmom laughed. "Isn't 'no comment' enough?"

"Not quite. I guess I'll be testing it out when I go apartment hunting."

"I don't think you'll have a problem," her stepmother said. "The news died down quickly. Apparently, people embezzling isn't a big story anymore."

She fluffed the pillow again.

"We're just glad you're okay." Her dad rose and gave her a hug. "We were worried. But we also think it will be nice to have you around for a few weeks. We're sorry a bed in the basement family room is all we have."

"It's fine, Dad. It's great, actually."

He squeezed her again. "Good. Stay as long as you want."

Warmth suffused her. She never doubted her dad's love. Just always believed he was too busy for her. "Thanks, Dad."

An unexpected knock at the door had everyone looking toward the stairway. "Who could be here at this time of night?"

Her stepmom said, "I'll get it."

"I'll come with you," her dad said. "We'll let Sophie get ready for bed."

She smiled. "Thanks."

She heard the muffled sounds of her parents talking to someone, then there was silence. This would have been the perfect time for a shower, but she hadn't had guts enough to go to the Montgomery and get her luggage. She didn't want to run into Wyatt. She wasn't ready to run into anybody yet. It was strangely wonderful to catch up with her dad and stepmom and two half siblings.

Luckily, her stepmom had some sweats she could borrow.

"Sophie?"

At the sound of Wyatt's voice, she spun around on the sofa bed. Her heart skipped a beat then she realized he was carrying one of her suitcases. Of course, he couldn't let something go undone. She'd said she'd pick up her suitcases, and since she hadn't, he was bringing them to her.

"Thanks for bringing my things," she said, trying not to sound tired and sad. She loved how he thought of everything, but there was a hole in his chest where a heart should be, and she had to remember that.

"I just brought this one case."

Detail guy Wyatt had forgotten something? "Really? Where are the other things?"

"In my condo?"

She stared at him. "Are you asking me or telling me?"

"Okay. They're in my condo." Carrying her overnight case, he walked down the steps. "Because I think you and I need to talk."

Oh, no. She wasn't going through that again. She'd cried enough to be dehydrated. They did not need to talk.

"I think we said everything that needed to be said when I got out of the limo."

He shook his head. "No. Well, yes. Maybe. At the time."

She frowned at him. He was never indecisive. Certainly never at a loss for words. His babbling was so out of character, she had no idea what to say.

"I have a couple of things I need to tell you."

Great. His side of the story. Just when she'd gotten herself to understand him in such a way that she could deal with the pain of losing him, he was about to muddy the waters.

Then it struck her that he was alone. A single dad with a baby and no nanny couldn't just go gallivanting in the middle of the night. "Where's Darcy?"

"I left her with Pete."

Her eyes widened. "The doorman?"

"The father of three. His shift was over. He agreed to watch her for a few hours while we straighten this out."

"I'm not going to be Darcy's nanny. I love her and I know I made a commitment, but I have to think of myself."

"Agreed."

She frowned. "You agree with me?"

"Yes."

"Then what do you think we need to straighten out?"

"I thought long and hard about what you said in the limo. I understand how difficult it would be for you to be Darcy's nanny. I even understood the part about you sleeping with your boss. Even though that's not quite how you said it. I believe you called yourself a dirty little secret."

She winced. "Thank you—I think."

"You're welcome. But the big thing I understood was that I don't have to be my parents."

Her heart stopped. This was new. "Okay."

"You're not hearing what I'm telling you. I spent most of today with Trace and Cade and realized we'll never stop being friends."

She frowned. "That's good."

He laughed. "It is good because it made me see that we're all masters of our own destiny— once I realized that, I also knew I feel the same way about you."

"That we'll always be friends?"

"That we can be anything we want." He took a quick breath. "I love having you around. My world is simply happier with you in it. Sophie, you were right. *I love you* and if I set my mind to loving you forever, I will."

Her heart brightened with hope, but she also

would never again misinterpret him. "You don't have to sound so surprised."

He laughed, but not like someone who was happy. Like someone who was relieved. "You're so wonderful. You're a partner. Someone I trust enough to confide in. Someone who can confide in me." He shook his head. "I can't explain it."

Her hopeful heart opened a bit. But just a bit. She heard what he was saying. She knew he meant it. But he'd hated the thought of commitment a little too staunchly to let it go so easily. And that was the thing keeping her from throwing herself into his arms.

"Don't you get it? I finally saw that I was holding myself back from something I really wanted and it was wrong. I saw you in my future and it was like the whole world opened up to me."

Tears formed in her eyes. She wished that meant he wanted what she wanted, but she'd said her piece and he'd rejected it. He had to be perfectly clear.

"Come home with me. But not as a friend or nanny or even the woman I love. As the woman I am committed to." He reached into his jacket pocket and pulled out a ring box. "Will you marry me?"

Gobsmacked, she stared at the biggest diamond she'd ever seen.

"Wow. I'd take it."

Sophie glanced over Wyatt's shoulder to see her dad and stepmom standing on the stairs, watching everything.

"Not because of the gorgeous ring," her stepmom quickly amended. "But because I think your guy is serious."

Wyatt caught her hands. "I am serious. I've never felt for anyone what I feel for you. Never wanted to share my life. But thinking of having you with me forever makes me incredibly happy."

Sophie glanced down at the ring. Now that her dad and stepmom were settled into their new house, there was a place for her with them. She wasn't desperate, but she loved Wyatt. More than she'd ever thought she could love anyone.

And her real place was with Wyatt and Darcy.

Especially since deep-thinker Wyatt wouldn't say any of this lightly.

"I love you, too."

"And you'll marry me?"

"I'll marry you."

Even as she said the words, Wyatt caught her around the waist and twirled her around.

Her dad and stepmom laughed. Apparently awoken by the commotion, her six-year-old half brother and five-year-old half sister appeared at the top of the steps.

Her brother said, "What's going on?"

Her dad laughed. "I think Sophie is getting married."

Her little sister gaped at her. "You're leaving?"

"Yeah." She grinned at them. "But I'll be back a lot for visits."

Both siblings ran down the steps and hugged her and she suddenly realized how lucky she was. She had a great dad, stepmom and half brother and sister. She'd been so afraid of disturbing their happiness, she hadn't even considered they might miss her too. If she hadn't desperately needed a place to stay, she might not have figured that out.

And she had Wyatt and Darcy.

She suddenly saw that the horrible thing her mother had done actually brought out the best in her life. She had Wyatt's love. She would be a mother to Darcy. Her dad and stepmom had found a place in her life, and all was right with her world.

EPILOGUE

THEY WAITED TWO years to get married. Cade and Reese tied the knot on his island. Marcia and Trace got married in Italy. Wyatt and Sophie said their vows at St. Patrick's Cathedral on Fifth Avenue.

She wore a gown created by a designer Wyatt's mother found. After months of hitting roadblocks with Wyatt about Darcy, his parents had had a real heart-to-heart talk with Wyatt, and his mother had decided that going with Wyatt's way of doing things was better than never seeing her granddaughter.

Sophie's stepmother had been with them every step of the wedding planning process. The three women had chosen cakes, bridesmaid dresses, centerpieces, tablecloths, lighting, silver, bouquets…and become unlikely friends. Even Wyatt's stuffy dad was coming around.

And no one had enrolled Darcy in preschool yet.

Now Sophie stood at the back of a very long

aisle, her hand tucked in her dad's arm, ready to walk to Wyatt and become his wife.

When her stepmom was seated and the last bridesmaid had taken the walk down the aisle, a hush fell over the church before the organ began to play Jeremiah Clarke's "Trumpet Voluntary."

She took the walk with her dad, who kissed her cheek and handed her over to Wyatt. The ceremony was solemn and elegant and when they walked out of the church Wyatt faced her.

"Well, we certainly can't break those vows."

She laughed and kissed him. "Yeah, they really made it feel extremely official."

He wrapped his hands around her waist. "Because it is. I wanted something like this because what I feel for you is special, important."

"It's not the nicest thing you've ever said to me, but I'll take it."

His face scrunched. "You keep track?"

"Not officially, but I remember things."

Bridesmaids, groomsmen and guests began spilling out the door to greet them. "What was the nicest thing I've ever said?"

She glanced at the growing crowd, stood on her tiptoes and whispered something he'd once said in bed.

He laughed heartily.

And their life together began officially. To have and to hold from this point forward.

With kids and goofy parents and enough money to enjoy it all, Sophie believed she'd found nirvana.

Especially since they'd bought the villa in Lake Como.

* * * * *

If you enjoyed this story,
check out these other great reads from
Susan Meier

Stolen Kiss with Her Billionaire Boss
Tuscan Summer with the Billionaire
The Billionaire's Island Reunion
Reunited Under the Mistletoe

All available now!